"Your brother's in a lot of trouble. I don't want to soft-pedal it to you."

"I know," Marissa said.

"But . . . I could put in a good word for him. I guess."

She could tell what that offer cost Clint, and her heart swelled. She was on her feet, her tears breaking through the dam. "That would be great. That's all I'm asking." Before she could consider her actions, she'd closed the space between them and put her arms around him. "He's not a bad person," she said, still sobbing. "You'll see when you meet him. You'll see."

Reluctantly, it seemed, Clint returned the embrace. He sifted her hair through his fingers and patted her back. "Don't cry, Marissa. I can't stand women crying."

"I'll t-try to stop." She pulled away slightly, embarrassed that her tears had made a damp spot on Clint's T-shirt. She was just so tired, that was all.

Clint looked down at her, then took her chin and tilted her face toward his. "Try a little harder, okay?" Then he touched his lips to hers. . . .

WHAT ARE *LOVESWEPT* ROMANCES?

They are stories of true romance and touching emotion. We believe those two very important ingredients are constants in our highly sensual and very believable stories in the LOVE-SWEPT line. Our goal is to give you, the reader, stories of consistently high quality that may sometimes make you laugh, sometimes make you cry, but are always fresh and creative and contain many delightful surprises within their pages.

Most romance fans read an enormous number of books. Those they truly love, they keep. Others may be traded with friends and soon forgotten. We hope that each LOVESWEPT romance will be a treasure—a "keeper." We will always try to publish

LOVE STORIES YOU'LL NEVER FORGET
BY AUTHORS YOU'LL ALWAYS REMEMBER

The Editors

THE DEVIL AND THE DEEP BLUE SEA

KAREN LEABO

BANTAM BOOKS
NEW YORK · TORONTO · LONDON · SYDNEY · AUCKLAND

THE DEVIL AND THE DEEP BLUE SEA
A Bantam Book / August 1998

ISBN 0-553-44694-0

Published simultaneously in the United States and Canada

Bantam Books are published by Bantam Books, a division of Bantam Dou-
bleday Dell Publishing Group, Inc. Its trademark, consisting of the words
"Bantam Books" and the portrayal of a rooster, is Registered in U.S. Patent
and Trademark Office and in other countries. Marca Registrada. Bantam
Books, 1540 Broadway, New York, New York 10036.

PRINTED IN THE UNITED STATES OF AMERICA

OPM   10 9 8 7 6 5 4 3 2 1

ONE

Clint Nichols sliced noiselessly through dark, murky water on a black night. The only way an uninvited guest could get into Houston's ultraexclusive Seville Yacht Club was through the water. Wearing a wet suit, his face blackened with greasepaint, he knew he was almost invisible. Still, he swam mostly underwater, surfacing as infrequently as possible.

Almost there, he thought, his lungs burning. His training at Quantico hadn't prepared him for anything like this. But he was in good shape—better than most of his younger colleagues. He worked like a demon to stay that way, especially since he'd hit forty.

The young Turks might think of him as a dinosaur, but he'd bet not one of them could make it through the grueling physical demands of this task. Too bad the only way he'd ever be able to brag about it was from a jail cell. The Bureau didn't exactly condone kidnapping and hijacking.

Clint carefully counted the boat slips. Most of them were occupied by empty sailboats and cabin cruisers. The wealthy owners paid tens of thousands for the crafts themselves, and thousands more to berth them at the prestigious Seville dock, then actually took them out only once or twice a year.

The whole thing was a pretentious waste of money in Clint's book. Then again, he'd never made enough money to think about owning anything fancier than his sixteen-foot catamaran, berthed in his garage. How could he understand what motivated rich men, men like Jimmy Gabriole?

At least Gabriole occasionally used his boat. He often arrived without his entourage, believing he was inviolable at the high-security yacht club. This particular weekend he'd brought his sister, Marissa, with him, providing Clint with the perfect opportunity. An eye for an eye.

A little sister for an ex-wife.

Jimmy had raised Marissa from the time she was ten and Jimmy was twenty, when their parents had been killed in a car bombing. Rumor had it that he valued her far more than any of his several wives over the years.

Slip 64. And there was *Fortune's Smile*, Gabriole's forty-two-foot cabin cruiser, not an ostentatious vessel by any means. Clint supposed that Gabriole didn't want to draw unwanted attention from the IRS. His official income was enough to allow him to live comfortably, but he wasn't a millionaire. Not unless you counted all the cash that came in under the table.

Fortune's Smile. Gabriole didn't know how ironic the name of his boat was. Fortune was about to frown on the

Mafioso. Big time. He'd find out what it felt like to have someone he loved disappear into thin air.

Clint found a vantage point behind a slime-covered pier and watched. The water was still a bit chilly on this late April night, and a soft rain was starting to fall, but Clint felt no discomfort. He was on a mission, and he had plenty of time. He wouldn't move until the optimum moment.

Clint had agonized for days about what to do. Rachelle, his sweet, wild little Rachelle, had been missing for almost a week, last seen at the Foxhunt, where she worked as a dancer. Police questioning had extracted no useful information. Clint's boss, Neil McCormick, had warned him to let it go. Rachelle was a minor player, and pursuing her fate might jeopardize an eight-month organized-crime investigation. Let the police handle it, he'd been told.

But Clint couldn't sit on his hands, not when it came to Rachelle. She'd briefly been his wife, and though their marriage had ended a long time ago, they still shared a bond. He looked out for her, bailed her out of scrapes now and then. And she provided him with useful bits of information. Her entire involvement with Gabriole and the Foxhunt had been Clint's idea. She'd risked her life for him. He could not abandon her now.

Clint pumped his legs beneath the water, trying to keep his circulation going. He didn't know when, or if, Marissa Gabriole would be left alone on the boat. But he would wait. He was good at waiting.

❦———————❦

"You're sure you don't want to come?" Jimmy asked his sister for the third time as he fastened a slim gold watch around his wrist. "I was supposed to show you a good time this weekend, and we haven't even left the dock."

"It's okay, Jimmy, really," Marissa Gabriole said, hoping she didn't look as green as she felt. She was actually relieved the lousy weather had prevented them from venturing out on Trinity Bay with *Fortune's Smile*. She loved her brother, and she'd been promising for a long time that she would spend a weekend on his sailboat with him and his wife, Sophia. Now that tax season was over, she'd run out of excuses, so this was the weekend. But sailing had never appealed to her. In fact, she'd discovered, much to her dismay, that she was prone to seasickness.

Since the weather had made sailing impossible this evening, Jimmy wanted to go out on the town.

"But it's lobster, Marissa," Sophia said. "How can you turn down a lobster dinner?" She pronounced the shellfish as "lobsta." Sophia was young and cute and unsophisticated, Jimmy's third wife. Still, Marissa couldn't help liking her. She was as ingenuous as a puppy.

"I just want to curl up in my bunk with a book," Marissa said. And some antacid. She'd downed a gallon of the pink stuff since her arrival at the Seville Yacht Club that afternoon. "Y'all go out and have fun. Don't worry about me, I'm fine."

"Okay, sissy," Jimmy said with a shrug. He'd never claimed to understand his sister's low-key ways. "We'll be back around midnight, maybe a little later."

Marissa breathed a sigh of relief as the hatch closed behind Jimmy and Sophia. She grabbed the edge of the fold-down galley table as the boat listed to one side, then the other, announcing the couple's disembarkment. Closing her eyes, she waited for the rocking to stop before she tried to walk.

What she really needed was some down time. This spring had been the busiest tax season ever for her growing accounting business. For weeks she'd been working twelve-hour days, seven days a week. Then, when the end had been in sight, Jimmy had shown up at her doorstep with a chicken-scrawled ledger book and a box of receipts, begging her to do a Schedule C for his restaurant, the Foxhunt. His regular bookkeeper had quit in a huff.

She'd done it because she had a hard time saying no to her older brother, who'd always done so much for her. But she'd barely finished the paperwork in time for Jimmy to make the April fifteenth tax deadline.

Thank God that insanity was over. Now all she wanted was to kick back, relax, be bored.

Marissa wiggled out of her sticky clothes. The sailboat didn't afford much privacy, so it was a relief to have the place to herself for a few hours. In deference to the muggy night, she wandered around in a beige silk camisole and paisley boxer shorts.

Some graham crackers and a glass of milk served as her dinner. After tidying up the tiny galley, then washing her face and brushing her teeth in a bathroom too small to turn around in, Marissa headed for her cozy—some might say cramped—quarters in the V-berth. She stretched out on clammy sheets and cracked open a mystery she'd been dying to read.

With a sigh, she decided that this wasn't paradise, but it wasn't half bad, either. No phone, no computer, no aggravations. Just the gentle sound of waves lapping against the hull, the murmur of a gentle rain, the occasional sleepy call of a water bird, and—

What was that noise? The boat abruptly leaned to one side, the way it did when someone boarded. Did Jimmy and Sophia forget something? It wasn't even ten o'clock. Maybe the weather had dissuaded them. It was supposed to be stormy later on.

She didn't hear any familiar voices. Tense with fear, Marissa put the book aside and felt around at the side of the mattress for her gun. Ever since she'd passed her test to carry a concealed weapon, she never went anywhere without her old Colt revolver.

It's a lady's gun, she remembered her father saying when he'd presented the weapon to her mother. Marissa had been seven or eight at the time. *Small, fits easily in the purse, but accurate. Not like some of them peashooters your bridge club friends carry.*

Her mother, who had never favored impractical furs or jewelry, had been pleased with the gift.

Now the gun belonged to Marissa. It was considered old-fashioned today, but she didn't care. She knew how to use it, and it would do the job if she ever had to pull the trigger, which she fervently hoped would never happen. She quickly loaded all six chambers from the box of ammunition in her overnight case.

The hatch at the opposite end of the boat rattled. Had

Jimmy locked it behind him? Probably. Jimmy took matters of security very seriously.

A loud creaking noise shattered the quiet. Oh, Lord, someone was breaking in! Marissa rolled onto her stomach, closed the privacy curtain that separated the V-berth from the rest of the boat, then trained her eye and the muzzle of her gun through a crack. If she could keep her presence a secret, she would. Maybe her uninvited guest would quickly canvass the main living area of the boat for valuables, then leave.

She could hope, anyway.

The hatch slowly lifted. Marissa held her breath as a silhouette descended the five steps that led into the living area of the boat. The man—and clearly, it was a man—wore a shiny black wet suit that outlined every sinew of his body. He looked hard and muscular, at least six feet tall. When his face came into view, Marissa saw that it was painted black, and she stifled a gasp. He looked like the bad guy from a James Bond flick.

Not your garden-variety boat breaker, then. Marissa became more frightened.

All right, where was she? Clint wondered as he descended the steps, grateful that someone had left a light on. He hoped Marissa was asleep. If she'd slept through his break-in, he stood a much better chance of avoiding injury to either of them while he subdued her. For intimidation purposes he had only a knife, so the element of surprise was essential.

Clint surveyed the boat's interior, taking a moment to

appreciate the tidy, space-efficient living area. Some designer had done a number on the place. The pale pastels, warm wood tones, and gauzy upholstery made the minimal space seem larger than it was. Ultramodern appliances in doll proportions defined the galley. He supposed there was some appeal to yachting. He could stand this for a few days.

Marissa was not in plain sight, nor in the tiny bathroom, which left the two sleeping cabins. He'd studied the plans for this model of boat, and he guessed that Gabriole and his wife would take the larger rear cabin, leaving Marissa the smaller V-berth, wedged into the prow.

That's where he headed, as quietly as possible.

A movement caught the corner of his eye. He jerked his head around, scanning the area, but didn't see anything. He was way too jumpy.

He continued toward the V-berth. He slid the curtains open.

He saw it, but he didn't believe it. Marissa Gabriole, her huge brown eyes filled with fear, lay on the bunk, pointing a gun at him.

"Freeze," she said calmly, deliberately. "Take one step closer and I'll pull the trigger."

He would have laughed if he hadn't been so scared. Who did she think she was with that ancient Colt pointed at his heart? Still, because the gun was old and the woman scared out of her wits didn't mean he couldn't be just as dead if she shot him.

"I'm not here to hurt you," he said softly, imagining

what a vision he must have presented her with his black-painted face.

"I don't care what your intentions are," she said. "Just leave the way you came."

He didn't have to think about what he did next. Years of training shaped his actions. With one lightning-quick motion he rotated his body, giving her the smallest possible target, and reached for the gun, deflecting the barrel away from him as he wrenched it out of her hand.

Marissa was propped on her elbows, so there was no way for her to react with any speed. The gun went from her grip to his in the blink of an eye, and she was left staring at Clint, first in disbelief, then with fear.

"You ought not to carry a gun unless you know how to use it," he said with a lazy drawl while he emptied the chambers, dropping the bullets to the floor. "For this very reason. Ten seconds ago I wasn't armed. Now I am."

"Spare me the lectures!" she said hotly. "I've had training. I have a license to carry a concealed weapon."

"Not trained well enough, obviously," he said, searching for a place to dispose of the gun. He thought briefly about keeping it for his own purposes, then rejected the idea. When he planned this operation, he'd promised himself he would do it without a gun. He didn't trust himself not to shoot Gabriole.

He opened a porthole and started to toss the revolver overboard.

"No!" Marissa objected.

He paused and looked at her.

"It was my mother's gun," she said almost sheepishly. "It has sentimental value. Don't throw it out. Please?"

Clint didn't believe her for a second, but he couldn't seem to make himself ignore her plea. Instead of pitching the gun out, he bent down, scooped up the bullets, and threw *them* out. He took a couple of steps backward into the galley and shoved the gun into a drawer. His gaze remained trained on Marissa.

He studied her then, really looked at her, and he had to admit he liked what he saw. Before, he'd seen her only at a distance. Other than coloring, she bore no resemblance to her short, stocky, snub-nosed brother. Marissa Gabriole had the face of a cosmetics model along with the eyes of a frightened fawn—an undeniably appealing combination. Her tousled hair was thick, shoulder length, gently curved under so the ends barely tickled her graceful neck. As for the rest of her . . .

"Put some clothes on," he said crossly, irritated that he was responding to her as a man. He didn't know much about Marissa other than that she was a Mafia princess, daughter of the late, great Lido Gabriole. But that was enough to disgust him. He shouldn't be attracted to such a person, no matter what his hormones thought of her.

At his terse command, Marissa had grabbed an oversize T-shirt from her bag and dragged it over her head. Clint breathed a sigh of relief. He wasn't sure how much longer he could have looked at her barely covered breasts without some noticeable reaction.

Now it was time to do something about his own attire. The wet suit was extremely uncomfortable. He unzipped it and peeled himself like a banana, conscious that Marissa's frightened gaze was riveted to him. When he was done, he wore only a pair of very brief swim trunks.

It hadn't occurred to him that his skimpy attire would be so awkward. He felt much too vulnerable with so much skin showing. Bare skin could all too easily be raked with fingernails. "Got another T-shirt I can borrow?" he asked as amiably as if they were friends at the beach.

Marissa visibly swallowed and licked her lips. She shoved her suitcase at him. "I think there's a blue one in there that might be big enough to fit you," she said grudgingly. "Otherwise, you can wear one of my brother's. His bag is in the other cabin." Her gaze never left him. "You know, he'll be back anytime. And he's not someone you want to mess with. He's got some pretty nasty friends. I'd leave if I were you. Really."

"I'm well aware of Jimmy's collection of friends. And I know he's dangerous. That's why I'm here." Clint sifted through pastel underthings—far more interesting to him than they should have been—before finding the blue T-shirt. He quickly donned the shirt. "I'm not planning to hurt you," he thought to add. Terrorizing women, even crime-family women, wasn't his goal. "If you'll just cooperate, we'll be done with this thing before morning."

"You're going to kill him," she said, her voice a monotone. "Oh, God, I knew someday they'd catch up with us."

"They?" Perhaps Marissa would prove to be a wealth of information.

"You," she clarified, malevolence burning from her eyes. "You're the one who killed our parents."

Marissa thought he was another gangster! All right, so maybe at this moment he wasn't acting like an FBI agent. But desperate circumstances called for desperate measures. He would do what he had to do to get Rachelle back safely—and if she was already dead, someone would pay.

Jimmy Gabriole. The man had featured prominently in all of Rachelle's info drops. He'd issued veiled threats against her. Clint had cautioned her to be careful, that giving herself away could lead to her death. But she'd become more and more reckless with her snooping into Jimmy's personal affairs.

Then she'd disappeared. Her apartment door had been bashed in, the furniture tossed about. He'd found no sign of Rachelle after days of searching.

Clint had a soft spot for Rachelle, never mind that she'd been unfaithful to him during their brief marriage, that she'd wiped out his bank account to buy drugs, that she liked to dance seminaked in front of strange men. There was an innate sweetness about her, a genuine desire to make the world a better place. He'd lost count of the number of excellent tips she'd given him, tips that led to arrests and convictions. None of her lowlife friends ever guessed that she had cooperated with the authorities.

Marrying her had been a huge mistake. He'd been younger then, more naive. After she took a bullet in a dark alley, a bullet meant for him, he'd been overwhelmed with gratitude. He could turn things around for her, he'd thought, give her a stable life. Rachelle had turned into his project.

He'd failed—miserably—to rehabilitate her, but he'd never, never stopped caring for her, feeling as if she were his responsibility.

Maybe she didn't live a sterling life, but she'd never

hurt anyone. She didn't deserve whatever Jimmy and his cohorts had done, or were planning to do, to her.

He shook off the dismal thoughts. Maybe his boss didn't think Rachelle's life was worth the effort it would take to find her, but Clint disagreed. Even if this caper got him into a lot of hot water, he owed it to Rachelle to do whatever it took.

"I've never killed anybody," he said to Marissa. "I'm not a criminal."

"Oh, right. That's why you broke in here looking like Al Jolson," she said with a brazen toss of her head. "What are you planning to do with the knife, slice up some mushrooms for pizza?"

She had nerve, he'd give her that. Most women in her position would by now have been reduced to trembling hysterics. She was trembling, a little, but she was not in the least hysterical.

He wanted to reassure her further, tell her the knife was for intimidation purposes and self-defense only. He wasn't about to kill someone in cold blood. But he didn't want his hostage to get too cocky. If she convinced herself he wouldn't hurt her, she might brazen her way out of the situation.

"If you cooperate, you won't get hurt. I'm not a criminal," he said again, realizing he sounded like Richard Nixon.

"Then why are you doing this?" Now she sounded scared, too scared to smart-mouth him further.

His conscience pinched him. Maybe some version of the truth would calm her. "Your brother made a good friend of mine disappear. I need a little leverage to convince him to tell me where she is."

"I don't think I understand."

He dispensed with the sugarcoating. "My friend learned a little too much about Jimmy's business dealings. Now she's gone. Do I need to draw you a picture?"

"You're saying Jimmy . . ." Marissa surprised Clint by laughing. "That's ridiculous. He can't even swat a fly without feeling guilty. If you believe he hurt your girlfriend, you've been sadly misinformed."

Clint shrugged. "Think what you will." If she deluded herself into believing Jimmy's hands were clean, that was her business. "Do you have a scarf, or maybe a pair of pantyhose in that bag of yours?"

"Why?" she asked warily.

"I have to tie you up. Sorry."

"You've already pawed through my things," she said, shoving the open duffel bag toward him with one delicate bare foot. Her toenails were painted a pearly pink, he noticed. "Help yourself."

Guiltily he riffled through her things again. He found a box of bullets, and his life flashed before his eyes. Who'd have thought she would carry a whole box with her? How many people did she plan on shooting over the weekend?

He'd almost made a costly mistake by not getting rid of Marissa's gun. She might have managed to get hold of the thing, reload it, and blow his head off.

Nonchalantly he took the box of bullets and tossed it out the porthole. It gave a satisfying *plop* as it hit the water.

She made no comment.

He selected, then discarded, a leather belt as a possible instrument of bondage. Finally he settled on a bra—lacy and shell pink, like her toenail polish. He idly wondered if she had panties to match.

"Turn around and face the wall," he ordered, his voice rough.

She obeyed, thank God. He wasn't sure what he would do if she resisted. Violence toward women wasn't one of his specialties.

"Cross your wrists behind you. Higher—yes, like that." As he knelt beside her on the bunk and tied her wrists together with a half hitch, he discerned the faint scent of peaches. Lord, the woman smelled like his aunt Aggie's peach orchard! Damn, she was turning him on. Of all the annoyances.

"Scoot over here." There were a couple of built-in drawers at the foot end of the bunk. He secured her wrists to one of the handles. "Is that comfortable?"

"Of course not," she snapped.

"Is it survivable for a few hours?"

"This is really going to take hours?"

"If we're lucky. If your brother comes through the way I think he will."

"What if I have to go to the bathroom?"

"We'll deal with it." That was one of the oldest tricks in the book, and he wasn't about to fall for it.

She sighed. "I suppose this won't cripple me for life or necessitate any amputations, but if you think it's comfortable, you try it."

"I'll take your word for it." He checked the bonds one

final time, resisting the urge to run a comforting hand down her bare arm. He doubted his touch would be the least bit comforting to her. "Now, any idea where the ignition key is?"

"You're going to *hijack* my brother's boat?"

"More importantly, I'm hijacking you." Jimmy probably wouldn't be easy to intimidate. He'd no doubt seen or been a part of his share of violence and threats, starting with the murder of his parents, which everyone knew was the result of some kind of gangland territorial dispute. He would not stand still while he thought Marissa was in danger. Jimmy Gabriole would either give Clint what he wanted . . . or kill him.

TWO

"Ignition key?" Clint repeated.

"I don't know," Marissa answered sullenly. Did he actually expect her to help him steal Jimmy's boat? "Jimmy probably keeps it with him. He's very security conscious."

"Afraid his own sister would steal his boat?" The hijacker grinned annoyingly.

"Afraid some lowlife would break in and steal it!" she corrected him. "How did you get in here, anyway?"

"That padlock on the hatch was child's play. Hotwiring a boat, though, that'll be a new experience. Are there any tools on board?"

"If I knew I wouldn't tell you where," she said.

Clint had to admire her fortitude. She was remarkably unintimidated by him, despite the fact that he looked like a rejected thug from central casting and she had no way of knowing he wouldn't actually harm her.

He made a cursory search for tools and found a toolbox in the hold with everything he would need to get the boat started. Now he had to worry about being seen. He would be above, drilling holes, in plain sight. The pier was nearly deserted—he'd noted that during his hours of observation—but occasionally people would stroll by, admiring the beautiful boats.

"Oh, for heaven's sake," Marissa said, "are you planning to drill holes and make a big mess?"

"Unless you can tell me any other way to get the engine started."

She hesitated. He apparently knew what he was doing, and Jimmy would be furious if his boat was damaged when he recovered it. "The ignition key is in the silverware drawer in the galley," she offered, still unsure if she was doing the right thing.

"Thanks. You don't by any chance have a cellular phone, do you?"

She sighed. He would see it sooner or later. "There's one right in front of your face, on the wall above the fridge."

"Oh. Thanks again. I appreciate the help."

"You're welcome," she said insincerely. Sheesh. A polite hijacker. She'd never heard of such a beast.

Marissa didn't see him for a while as he ran about above deck untying lines, pulling up bumpers. She kept hoping that somehow, someone would put a stop to this insanity. Then the engine started, and the boat eased away from the dock, on its way to who knew where, and her hopes for an easy resolution turned to flotsam.

To distract herself from her roiling stomach, which did not care for the bumpy ride, she thought about the hijacker's accusations against Jimmy. Lord, what had her brother gotten himself involved in this time? He was always claiming that he'd gone straight, that he was running a legitimate business or holding a real job. But time and time again, he got sucked in by the lure of easy money—usually some scheme instigated by his "friend" Eddie Constantine.

She had to face the fact that Jimmy was a weak man when it came to money, and women, and food, and booze. But—and this was an important distinction—he didn't have a mean bone in his body. He never even got angry. Marissa had meant what she told the hijacker. If some woman had turned up missing, killed, or kidnapped, Jimmy wasn't responsible. He might flirt with the edges of organized crime, but he wouldn't delve deep enough to be privy to murder and mayhem.

She supposed that was why she'd never been able to turn her back on him. No matter what else he did, he cared for people, especially her. He was even nice to his ex-wives!

Marissa looked out the porthole. Through the rain droplets she could see the lights of the many restaurants that lined the exit channel from Clear Lake into Trinity Bay . . . then Galveston Bay . . . then the Gulf of Mexico. My God, where was he taking her? Oh, why hadn't she gone with Jimmy and Sophia? She could be sitting in one of those restaurants now, sipping a margarita.

The boat made a particularly dramatic swoop as it crested a swell. The farther out in the channel they went, the rougher the sea became. Pretty soon it would be a roller-coaster ride. Marissa didn't know if her stomach could make it. She wondered how long they would be out on the water.

On deck, Clint was wishing he'd kept his wet suit on. The rain came down in earnest now. That and a generous amount of salt spray from the rough waters had soaked him through to the skin. The stormy weather didn't bother him—he'd been negotiating these waters since he was big enough to sail a Sunfish, and he'd survived some hellish storms. But he hated being cold and wet. He hoped like hell that Rusty remembered to bring everything Clint had asked for, which included a change of clothes and a proper pair of handcuffs.

Clint concentrated on staying between the red and green flags that delineated the channel. He had the water to himself—no other idiot would be crazy enough to go out in such weather. He hoped Rusty wasn't having any problems with his boat. Rachelle's brother had decent boating experience, but he was only twenty-five. Clint could remember having a lot more chutzpah than brains at that age.

He was unutterably relieved when he saw the five-mile buoy that marked the agreed-upon rendezvous point, just far enough into Trinity Bay to avoid witnesses. He'd used the Gabrioles' cellular phone to alert Rusty, who was standing by for his call, that the operation had launched successfully. They'd agreed to meet between eleven-thirty and midnight.

Clint checked his diving watch. He was early, and it seemed as if the rain might be easing up. Maybe there was a God after all. He pulled to the side of the channel and dropped anchor, hoping Rusty wouldn't be too long.

It was time to check on his pretty little hostage. Clint opened the hatch and descended, surprised to hear moaning. Oh, Lord, what now? "Marissa?" He made his way as quickly as he could to the V-berth. The boat made a violent pitch, sending him sprawling against the galley table. Damn, he'd have a bruise there tomorrow to match the other thirty-seven he had.

"Marissa?" he called again, whisking back the curtain.

She was right where he'd left her . . . but she didn't look too good.

"What's wrong?" he demanded.

"Oh, just let me die." Her eyes were closed, her head thrown back, and beads of perspiration dotted the ivory skin of her forehead and upper lip, though it was not warm in the cabin.

Then it hit him. She was seasick! Her color was actually more celery than ivory. Maybe fresh air would help. He opened the porthole, letting in some damp, cool air. "You're not going to throw up, are you?" he asked with trepidation. If she did, in her current position she would . . . no, it didn't bear thinking about.

"Yes," she answered him. "Any moment."

"Oh, *Jeez.*" He wasted no time untying the pink bra that bound her hands to the drawer handle. There were ugly red marks around her wrists, he saw, feeling a twinge of guilt.

"Oh, thank you, thank you," she said as she wiggled past him.

"Wait a minute." He was in instant pursuit, wondering if this might be a ploy. Would she lunge for a kitchen knife? He grabbed her arm, so at least he would have some control over her. He didn't believe she could overpower him, but a frightened woman with a frying pan or a steam iron was a force to be reckoned with.

"Fresh air. I have to go on deck," she said.

"No!" What if she jumped overboard? If she was a strong swimmer, she could make it to land. And if she wasn't, she would drown. Neither prospect was desirable. He grabbed one of her ankles even as she was pushing up the hatch.

"Let me go!"

"You can't go up there. It's . . . dangerous. If you'll just look out the porthole at the horizon, you'll feel better."

"I have to get outside!" She gave a mighty kick backward with her free foot, which landed squarely on Clint's nose.

He yowled and released her; she made good her threat and hopped out on deck. He was right behind her, but as it turned out, there was no need for him to worry. She headed straight for the railing, leaned over it, and lost the contents of her stomach.

The poor woman, he thought, then caught himself. She was a Mafia princess, and she'd just kicked him in the face, probably broken his nose if his luck was running true. She wasn't some delicate hothouse flower. But she was really, really sick.

The torrential rain quickly soaked through Marissa's clothes and turned her hair into dark, glossy ropes. Clint put his arm around her, more to keep her from being jostled overboard than out of concern for her condition. He noticed the warmth of her body, the softness of her skin, even the smell of her rain-soaked hair. And when she straightened up, her nipples were clearly visible through the wet T-shirt she wore.

Clint felt an unmistakable tension in his groin and had to stifle a groan. He didn't need this—this adolescent reaction to a pretty woman. In his skimpy attire, it wouldn't be difficult to see, although Marissa was probably too sick to take notice.

"C'mon, you can't stand out here in the rain all night," he said.

She was leaning against him, her eyes closed, breathing in great gulps of air. "Leave me out here. Maybe a wave will wash over the boat and take me with it when it leaves. Put me out of my misery."

"No, no, that won't do," he said in his most cajoling voice. "I need a live, healthy hostage if I'm going to negotiate with your big brother. Come on, one foot in front of the other."

"The boat's too stuffy," she complained, leaning her head on his shoulder. But she began moving toward the hatch.

"We'll unstuff it—open some windows, turn on the AC."

She stopped, grabbing a handle for support. "What if I have to get sick again?"

"We'll find you a basin. You can't stay out here. It's dangerous."

"I think going below with you is dangerous," she

groused, proving that she wasn't so sick she didn't appreciate her situation.

"Nonsense. I'm a pussycat once you get to know me." Basically, he was telling the truth. Until a couple of hours before, he'd been the soul of virtue, the consummate FBI agent—long hours, nose to the grindstone, everything through the proper channels. In fourteen years with the Bureau, he'd never driven Bureau cars for personal use, he didn't drink or get involved in sex scandals.

He'd been saving it all up for now, he guessed.

"Pussycat? A big, nasty panther, is more like it," Marissa said. At least she'd stopped groaning, and she felt well enough to argue. Once they were back inside the boat, where there was some light, he could see she had a little color in her face other than green. But she was also shivering.

"Why don't you put on some dry clothes?" he suggested.

"Mmm, too much effort." She collapsed into one of the built-in banquettes in the galley dining area. "Can't you stop this boat from pitching?"

"I'm good, but I'm not that good." He searched around until he found a small trash can. He emptied it into a larger receptacle in the galley, then handed the smaller can to Marissa. "Here. No more trips on deck, okay? You scared me half to death. I thought you were going to throw yourself overboard."

"I considered it." She leaned back and closed her eyes, calm for the moment. "Do you think you could fetch the stomach medicine from my bag?"

"Dramamine is what you need. You don't have any?"

"No. I didn't think to bring that. I've never been prone to seasickness before. Maybe Jimmy or Sophia has some. When Sophia—my brother's wife—travels, she brings everything that's not nailed down. You know, she wouldn't be caught dead without matching purse and shoes."

"I'll check around." Clint knew he ought to tie Marissa up again. But as sick as she was she hardly seemed much of a threat.

He dug around in the suitcases he found in the main sleeping cabin, finding all kinds of intriguing items, including lots of black lingerie and a pair of handcuffs. The handcuffs brought him only a moment of satisfaction; they were the play kind that didn't really lock. As for the lingerie, if he had to paw through women's underwear, he'd have preferred Marissa's dainty pastels.

In a zippered leather case inside Jimmy's duffel bag, he hit pay dirt—a package of generic travel sickness medication. It would have the added benefit of making Marissa drowsy, thus easier to handle. Not that she was all that difficult right now. She'd been fairly cooperative from the beginning, something he sorely appreciated.

On the other hand, the fear had gone out of her eyes too. She knew he wouldn't hurt her, and that could make her more dangerous. He'd better keep an eye on her.

He brought her two of the pills and a glass of water. She eyed them suspiciously, then looked back up at him. "I'm supposed to take these?"

"I got them from your brother's case," he said. "Do you want to see the package they came from?"

She shook her head, grimaced, and downed the medicine. That's when Clint noticed that her shivering was worse. He got a blanket from the V-berth and tucked it around her, taking longer with the task than was necessary. He liked touching her, and an unexpected wave of protectiveness washed over him as she lay down on the banquette and snuggled under the blanket, far too trusting of him. Her bare feet poked out, and he covered them up. Those pearly-pink toenails were killers.

Clint went back on deck. The waves were so bad now, they were actually breaking over the side of the boat. Where was Rusty? Surely he hadn't wimped out because of the weather. Rusty liked to race motorcycles and play chicken with freight trains. A little rain and wind wouldn't deter him.

Maybe the lousy weather had merely delayed him. It was slow going through these waves, even for an experienced sailor.

Clint kept one eye on his hostage, who was sleeping peacefully, and one eye out the hatch. If Rusty didn't show in another few minutes, Clint would be forced to move to plan B, which meant he would have to beach *Fortune's Smile* someplace out of the way and proceed on foot with his hostile companion to some safe haven where he could carry out the rest of his scheme. The circumstances wouldn't be ideal, but he couldn't stay where he was indefinitely. Jimmy Gabriole could even now be reporting his missing boat and sister to the police and the Coast Guard.

He worked out the logistics in his head, using every minute of FBI training and experience under his belt to weight the pros and cons of his contingency plan, figuring the odds of his finding someplace to hole up without arousing suspicion. They weren't very high.

Just when he was about to decide he had to act on plan B, he heard a muffled honking noise, sort of a cross between a car horn and a lovesick walrus. Was it Rusty, or some intrepid shrimp boat warning him to get out of the way?

He climbed through the hatch to the deck. The rain had let up again, but the wind was incredible, and cold. Sure enough, coming down the channel was a decrepit-looking fishing boat, small by shrimping standards and apparently not very seaworthy. Clint could barely make out the boat's name, hand-painted in shaky letters: *Phen-Hu*.

When someone on the other boat shined a searchlight in his direction, he waived a friendly greeting so they wouldn't think he was in distress and report him to the Coast Guard.

Instead of chugging on past him, though, the boat slowed, reversed, then angled toward him.

Oh, no. Rusty wouldn't have . . . couldn't have. Clint had told him exactly where to go to rent a boat, whom to talk to, what type of boat to get, what story to tell. He'd provided cash for the transaction. And Rusty shows up with this—this atrocity?

"Haloo!" a voice called on the wind. Rusty's voice.

Clint shuddered. The *Phen-Hu* looked like one good wave would sink it. What had Rusty been thinking? Well, hell, they were stuck with the decision now. Clint couldn't afford to spend any more time aboard Gabriole's boat.

With the swells at six feet, it took forever to get the two boats close enough so that Rusty could throw out a catchable line. Clint snagged the rope on their third attempt.

Even then, pulling the boats together wasn't easy. Every gust of wind, every wave, conspired to keep the crafts apart. And when they did meet, they hit with alarming force.

Clint couldn't afford to waste any time. He had to get Marissa on board the *Phen-Hu*, then untether the two boats before they bashed each other to bits. He doubted his hostage would cooperate—especially when she saw the appearance of her destination boat. More rust than paint, the *Phen-Hu* was downright alarming.

Rusty had climbed down from his perch in the cockpit. "You got the package?" he called to Clint.

"Sure do." And she was sound asleep. He hated the thought of dragging Marissa out in the wind and rain, but it had to be done. "Get ready to help me cross over." Even in calm waters, jumping from one boat to another with a woman over his shoulder would be a trick.

He went back down into the main cabin. Marissa was curled into a ball beneath the blanket, her head pillowed against her folded hands, her hair draped across her face. The dark lashes were stark against her pale cheeks. He felt an unwelcome stab of responsibility for her, something he hadn't anticipated. He'd thought he would feel nothing for her but revulsion.

Revulsion was the farthest thing from his mind.

With a sigh he scooped her into his arms. She was a petite woman, thank goodness, but still an awkward package when it came to climbing the stairs through the tiny hatch. He put her over his shoulder, fireman-style. Everything was going well until she woke up . . . in a panic.

"What? What are you doing?" she screamed, beating his back with her fists. She packed a pretty good wallop. With more hysteria than she'd shown all evening, she asked, "You're throwing me overboard?"

"Pipe down," Clint said irritably. "If I were bent on drowning you, I could have done that earlier. I'm just moving you to another boat."

His reassurances didn't stop her struggling. "Put me down!"

"It'll be easier this way, trust me."

"Trust you? Right. I don't even know your name."

And she wouldn't, if he had anything to say about it.

"Oh, my God. Is that the boat I'm going on?"

"Yup."

"It's sinking!"

"It's not sinking." Although it was listing decidedly to starboard. He hoped that was an optical illusion, due to the boats being tied together.

"No, I don't want to go on that boat. I refuse! You're going to drown both of us!" Now Marissa was kicking in addition to the arm flailing and fist pounding.

"You keep that up, and I'm liable to drop you between the boats."

"Why not? Why don't you put some cement boots on me and get it over with? Isn't that what you gangsters do?" She finally did stop struggling.

Gangsters. Clint longed to tell her that he wasn't the

gangster in this scenario. Her brother had started this. If Jimmy had left Rachelle alone, Clint wouldn't have resorted to such reprehensible behavior. But he couldn't tell Marissa that. If by some miracle he came through this thing with his identity unknown, he didn't want Marissa turning around and blabbing to the police or the media any clues about him. He might still preserve his job.

Although, sometimes, he wasn't sure he wanted it anymore.

Hanging on to lines and awnings and anything that appeared as if it might give support, Clint staggered to the railing. There was a good five-foot gap between the boats when they pulled apart. "Can't you pull them closer together?" Clint called to Rusty.

"Just jump."

"With a hundred and ten pounds across my shoulder?"

"Hand her over here, then." Rusty held out his arms.

Clint resisted that idea, though he wasn't sure why. Maybe he simply didn't trust Rusty to keep Marissa under control. Or maybe he didn't want the other man putting his hands on her. Rusty might not have the same degree of respect for their hostage as Clint did.

Visions of dropping Marissa into the inky blackness of the water filled his mind, increasing his uneasiness. But he had to do this—and he could, if he timed it right. The two boats were habitually bumping together and pulling apart. There was a rhythm to it. He waited, counting, then made a leap just as the two railings came together. He landed in a stinking pile of ropes on the other boat.

He'd taken most of the blow himself, shielding

Marissa as they'd hit the deck. Now he had a sore shoulder *and* a sore nose. But was she grateful? Of course not.

"Pee-yuuu, this place stinks to high heaven," she complained. "You take someone who's seasick and toss her onto a pile of rope that smells like dead fish?"

Clint stood and pulled Marissa to her feet in a hurry. He didn't want her hurling again. But now that he thought about it, she didn't sound sick anymore. Those pills must've done their job.

As she fought with the blanket that was still wrapped around her, Clint scooped her into his arms. She was one feisty lady. He would have to tie her up again.

"Hey, what are you doing?" she asked.

"Taking you somewhere dry."

"Why isn't she tied up?" Rusty wanted to know.

"It's a long story. And where did you get this pile of excrement you call a boat?"

"I got such a deal," Rusty said enthusiastically as he followed Clint through a doorway into a dark, dank interior that smelled even more strongly of fish. Clint guessed this was where the fishermen stored their catch. "The *Phen-Hu*'s crew didn't want to take her out in this weather," Rusty continued. "I gave them less than half what we would have paid for one of them fancy yachts like you wanted me to rent. And if we don't return it— hey, who's gonna believe a bunch of fishermen who can't speak English?"

Clint found his new partner's logic almost as nauseating as the fish smell. Money wasn't the issue here, didn't he get that? Neither was stealing some family's means of support. "We'll be lucky if this tank lasts through the night," he lashed out. "Next time I tell you to go to a certain place and rent a certain boat, just do it, okay?"

"Hey, who says I gotta follow your orders? I'm not one of your fibbie lackeys. We're in this together, equal partners."

Then why had Clint provided the plan, the provisions, and the money? He decided arguing with Rusty was futile at this point. Many a criminal operation had fallen apart because of infighting among the perpetrators.

"Yeah, yeah, equal partners," he said wearily. "Did you bring all the stuff I asked for?"

"Of course I did. I'm not an idiot, Clint."

Clint cringed at the use of his name but made no comment. "Why don't you cut us loose, and let's see what this bucket of bolts can do?" he suggested. As soon as they were a safe distance away, he would make his first call to Jimmy. Rusty *better* have brought the special, untraceable cellular phone Clint had "borrowed" from the office.

Marissa, who had stood stock still since Clint set her down in the hold, spoke up. "I'd rather sit out on deck than stay in this disgusting place," she groused. "And what did your friend mean by 'fibbie'? That's jargon for FBI, isn't it?"

Terrific, just terrific. Clint was beginning to believe he'd made a terrible mistake by putting his trust, however limited, in his ex-brother-in-law.

THREE

Marissa's stomach had calmed down. But she was cold and wet, she'd left everything familiar behind, her kidnapper had met up with a partner who *really* frightened her, and, perhaps worst of all, when the police finally found her, dead or alive, she would be wearing paisley boxer shorts and a clashing red T-shirt.

She should have changed her clothes, but at the time she had the opportunity, she'd been feeling too sick to worry about fashion sense. If she'd only known how vulnerable and uncomfortable she would feel running around in her underwear! At least she had the blanket, soggy though it was.

Her kidnapper had tied her up again, but at least he'd taken her out of the fishy hold and up to the cockpit. She had both wrists loosely tied to a strut that supported the canopy, but she still had enough freedom of movement so she could keep her balance when the waves hit. She was actually starting to get the hang of anticipating the boat's bucks and swoops, and her seasickness was completely gone.

Now she could devote herself to figuring out who her captors were and what they were trying to accomplish. She'd already learned some valuable information. The first guy, her kidnapper, was an FBI agent or former agent, and his name was Clint. His partner had referred to him by that name once, much to Clint's displeasure.

She didn't know the other guy's name, but for some reason he frightened her much more than Clint did. He was younger—in his twenties, Marissa guessed—and seemed more reckless, less focused. He looked on her as an object, a means to an end, rather than as a human being. As roughly as Clint had treated her, she got the feeling that he didn't really want to hurt her, that he'd rather be home in bed asleep than perpetrating a crime.

His partner, on the other hand, was enjoying himself.

As for their motive for kidnapping her, she didn't believe this fairy tale Clint had spun about a missing woman. It made no sense. Maybe he was covering up a cruder reason for this ridiculous production—greed. He was holding her for ransom.

Jimmy didn't have as much money as he led people to think. Actually, because of careful investing over the years, Marissa's share of their parents' legacy was a lot healthier than Jimmy's. Why didn't her captors ask *her* for ransom money? She'd give it to them.

But why would some FBI agent be kidnapping for ransom? For Clint, at least, this operation felt distinctly personal. That thought made her frown with distaste. Was she part of some vendetta?

The idea made her shiver more than the cool, misty wind. Revenge was a powerful motivator; she knew first-hand. She'd always feared, perhaps irrationally, that whoever had killed her parents would someday come back for her.

"Where are we going?" she asked Clint as he passed by. Rusty was at the helm, whooping with glee every time the *Phen-Hu* plowed through a huge wave, sending rooster tails of water through the air and sometimes onto the three people on board.

"You don't need to know," he said gruffly as he stared at a cellular phone. "How come your brother isn't answering his page?"

So he was calling Jimmy. If Jimmy wasn't returning the page, Clint probably didn't have his private pager number. He carried two—one for public use, and one for a select few people. Did she dare give it to Clint?

She decided she might as well. The sooner he got hold of Jimmy, the faster this plan would proceed. Clint had said a few hours, by morning at the latest. She hoped that was true.

"I'll give you another number to try," she said, shouting above the roar of the *Phen-Hu*'s sick-sounding engine.

Clint raised his eyebrows. "Really?"

"Yes." She realized that since he'd washed the black off his face, he was kind of handsome, in a devilish way. Dark hair, dark eyes, eyebrows that slashed straight across his face—unless something piqued his interest. Then those eyebrows quirked and wavered all over the place—first one raised, then the other, then both pointed downward in a scowl, or elevated in feigned innocence.

Well, his looks were irrelevant, she decided. Kidnappers came in all shapes and sizes. A good-looking one wasn't necessarily any less lethal.

He handed her the phone.

"Can't they trace the call?" she asked.

"It's difficult to trace a cellular phone. Anyway, this one's untraceable."

She raised her eyebrows. "An FBI toy?"

He didn't answer.

She punched in Jimmy's private number, then handed it back. Clint listened, punched in another number, then hung up. "We'll see. What time did you expect him back on the boat?"

"Before now." It was after one-thirty.

"Damn. I sure as hell wanted to catch him before he called the cops."

Marissa didn't say anything, but the chances of Jimmy calling the cops were slim to none, unless he was positive the theft of his boat and the kidnapping of his sister weren't related to the organization. The people Jimmy hung around with didn't like police involvement for any reason. Men had been known to die for bringing authorities in at inconvenient times.

If only Jimmy would steer clear of those bad-apple friends of his. But to Jimmy, friendship—belonging, being an accepted part of the gang—was more important than just about anything else.

Clint's phone rang. He flipped it open nervously. "Yeah?"

"Is it him?" Marissa asked.

"Shh!" The younger man, the one driving the boat,

held up a hand to silence Marissa. He was tense, his knuckles white around the steering wheel. "What's he say?"

"Mr. Gabriole," Clint said in acknowledgment, "I have someone here you should talk to." He held the phone up to Marissa's ear.

"Jimmy? Where are you?"

"Never mind me. What's wrong, sissy?"

She tried her best to curb the sudden wave of hysteria that threatened. She had to communicate as much information as possible while she had the chance. "A guy broke into your boat. He stole it and took me with him."

"My boat?"

"Jimmy, I've been kidnapped! Listen to what they have to say."

"Have they hurt you?" he bellowed.

"No, not yet. I'm on the *Phen*—" Clint had jerked the phone away before she could tell Jimmy the name of the boat. Fast reflexes, she thought.

"Did you hear that? I've got your precious Marissa, and if you want her back in one piece, you'll pay close attention."

Marissa shuddered. Clint's voice sounded different when he talked to Jimmy, harsher, meaner. He didn't sound like the same man who had held her while she was sick, murmuring words of comfort.

"I'm looking for a woman," Clint said. "Rachelle Pierce. You know who she is, and you know where she is." There was a pause. Then Clint said, "I'm going to give your memory a chance to improve. Unless you'd like for me to forget your sister's name and what I did with her, your memory *will* improve. Meanwhile, don't even think about calling the cops, or you'll never see Marissa alive again. Oh, and by the way, your sister's a nice-looking woman. The longer I have her, the more tempting she gets, understand?" He hung up with a curse.

The younger man laughed, a high-pitched giggle that one might expect to hear in a psych ward.

Marissa thought she might be ill again. She ducked into the shadows and tried to be invisible, but she kept a wary eye on Clint. He wouldn't really touch her, would he?

"Oh, don't look at me like that," Clint barked. "I already told you, I'm not going to hurt you."

"You said you wouldn't hurt me *if* Jimmy cooperated. So far he hasn't."

"He will."

"But if he doesn't?"

"I won't hurt you," Clint repeated. "But Jimmy doesn't have to know that. My plan won't work unless he thinks you're in mortal danger."

"And then he'll tell you where this woman, this . . ." What name had he mentioned? "This Rachel is."

"Her name's Rachelle. And yes, that's the general plan."

Marissa shook her head. "You're barking up the wrong tree. I have no doubt that your girlfriend disappeared, and maybe Jimmy knew her—"

"She worked for him. At his club."

"Okay, whatever. What I'm trying to tell you is, if she was hurt or kidnapped or whatever, Jimmy didn't do it. He is not that kind of man. I've known him for thirty years, and he is a kind person, even if he has some not-so-nice friends."

"Yeah? Tell me about these friends."

Marissa immediately realized she'd said too much. If this guy really was a Fed, he might be angling for evidence that would help him put Jimmy in jail. And Jimmy didn't deserve that. Yeah, he got involved in some illegal gambling schemes. He probably fudged a little on his income taxes, though Marissa knew nothing for sure. She did know he gave jobs to people without checking credentials and paid them in cash. So did millions of other employers.

"I'm not in a chatty mood."

Clint's eyes narrowed. "You ought to get chatty where Jimmy's concerned. Help me figure out how to get what I want from him. Or this is going to be a long ordeal for both of us."

The rain had started up again. Clint studied Marissa. She looked miserable, and her arms were probably starting to hurt, tied in that raised position. He decided he couldn't leave her that way.

He was aiming the *Phen-Hu* for open water, then up the Texas coast. He planned to beach her at the first opportunity. But at the rate they were going it would take all night to clear Galveston Bay.

He had an idea. "Marissa?"

"Yes?" She looked at him with blazing eyes.

"I found a place where you can lie down. There are

some wooden bunks below. It's pretty primitive, but at least you'd be out of the wind."

She nodded, her angry gaze faltering. He unfastened the ties at her wrists, then walked her around to starboard where a hatch led belowdecks. She balked at the entrance. "It's dark. There could be rats or God-knows-what down there."

"There's a light." Clint released her briefly and preceded her down the hatch, hoping she didn't get it into her head to kick him from behind. But he guessed that she wouldn't want to incapacitate the only person on the boat with any navigational abilities. Surely she was smart enough to figure that out.

He groped around and finally came up with the chain to the bare bulb hanging from the ceiling.

Marissa peered in, then followed Clint down the stairs. "I don't know about this."

"It's dry, and the fish smell isn't so bad." He took her arm and led her to one of the old-fashioned bunks, which swung down from the wall on chains. Using the old hank of rope he'd brought with him, he secured her wrist to one of the planks in the bunk. "There, you can lie down if you want."

Marissa tried, using her trusty blanket to pillow her head. "Hmm, it's not terrible."

"Good. You want to take another motion-sickness pill, just in case?"

"You brought them with you?"

"Yeah. The package is a little soggy, but I think the pills are okay."

"Leave 'em with me. Right now, I'm feeling okay."

Clint was unutterably relieved. He'd been worried about her, probably more than he should have been. He felt a silly urge to stay with her, to watch over her while she fell asleep, but he resisted. He couldn't leave Rusty in charge of the helm for too long. Rachelle's brother knew next to nothing about steering a boat this size.

The rain was falling in sheets by the time Clint returned to the cockpit. Rusty was standing in front of the wheel, doing his Captain Ahab imitation. A cigarette dangled from his lips. Clint couldn't imagine how the thing stayed lit, given the dubious protection of the tattered canopy.

"Man, I didn't know she'd be such a babe," Rusty said. "You getting any action?"

"No," Clint snapped.

"Yeah, I don't blame you. You're gonna be in enough trouble for snatching Jimmy the Gab's sister. If you bopped her, he'd come after you with an ax."

"How do you know so much about Jimmy?" Clint asked.

"Rachelle. She's a blabber. You know how she is."

"I don't suppose she ever told you exactly what she'd found out about Jimmy, did she?"

Rusty shook his head. "When it came to working for you, she kept her mouth shut. Absolutely. I don't know, man, it's like you cast a spell on her. She'll screw everybody else ten ways to Sunday, but she's always been completely loyal to you, even after the divorce." Rusty laughed again, that high-pitched giggle that gave Clint the willies.

A bolt of lightning ripped across the sky, followed by a

loud clap of thunder. Until now, the storms had been more remote, but it looked as if they were heading directly into one now. The waves were getting worse, the rain harder.

"Turn on the radio," Clint said. "See if you can get a weather report."

"I already tried," Rusty said offhandedly. "Radio's busted."

"The radio's broken?" Good Lord, what if they got into trouble? Calling the Coast Guard would land them in jail, but that was better than drowning. "That's just great, Rusty. How much fuel we got?"

"Uh, don't know that, either. Fuel gauge doesn't work. But they told me the tank was full when they turned over the boat to me, and it's got a big fuel tank. We'll be okay."

Clint barely managed to keep his hands from around the young man's throat. There were enough unknown elements, enough risks associated with this operation even if the whole thing went like clockwork. To add additional risks was unthinkable to his FBI-trained mind. Yet Rusty had thought it clever to rent this piece of garbage.

Well, Rusty was hardly more than a kid, Clint reminded himself. He'd had no training of any kind. Clint was used to working with the best-trained law enforcement minds in the world. He was spoiled. The boat was working out so far.

That's when the *Phen-Hu* bucked as if they'd hit a rock. The engine made a horrific noise, grinding and coughing. Finally it went silent.

"What the hell?" Rusty screamed. "I didn't do it, I swear. I steered right where you told me to."

"Take it easy, dude. I didn't say you did it." Clint peered over the back of the boat. Even in this weather, it was easy to see what the problem was. A tree—not just a branch, but an entire uprooted tree—was stuck in one of the boat's huge props. Either the engine had shut itself off to avoid burning up . . . or it had burned up.

"Where are the life jackets?" he asked Rusty.

Rusty shrugged. "Maybe in there?" He pointed to a wooden storage container. It was padlocked.

"Just what I needed," Clint muttered. The lock looked flimsy enough. After a couple of good yanks, it gave way.

Inside the box, which stunk to high heaven, he found two of the most pitiful-looking life jackets he'd ever seen. It looked as if rats had been chewing on them. A pair of small, yellow eyes glowed at him from the depths of the bin, confirming his suspicions. With a shudder of distaste he grabbed one of the jackets, shook it to make sure it didn't have any unwanted residents on it, and fastened it around his neck.

"What are you doing?" Rusty asked skeptically.

"I'm going into the water to get rid of that tree in the propeller," Clint answered. "I want you to be ready to throw me a line in case I lose my hold on the boat." This was a distinct possibility. The waves were big enough to surf.

"Okay."

The two men climbed down to the main deck. Rusty grabbed a coil of rope, and Clint found the ladder that descended the boat's stern. The wind was blowing so hard, it was a challenge to hang on. Eventually he was forced to abandon the ladder and jump the rest of the way into the water. He grabbed a handhold for support, but he found that with the boat bucking up and down, he couldn't maintain his grip. He hoped Rusty could throw a rope with some degree of accuracy.

Clint grabbed a propeller blade and tried to push the tree loose with his feet. It was like a stalk of celery stuck in a food processor blade. It gave a little bit. He kept working at it, knowing that even if he succeeded in dislodging the tree, the propeller blades were most likely bent, the engine burned up. But he had to try. The thought of floating around in the middle of the bay with a dead engine and no radio, not to mention a shortage of life jackets, wasn't pleasant.

Marissa awoke with the taint of smoke in her nose. She realized that somehow she'd fallen asleep on the hard wooden bunk even with her arm secured to a slat in a hideously uncomfortable position. Her arm was tingling from lack of circulation, but that was the least of her worries. The cabin was laced with wisps of smoke, her visibility rapidly decreasing as the smoke thickened.

Fire. "Fire!" she yelled, her words a split second behind the realization. But what were the chances of either of her captors hearing her above the racket of the storm? Even without looking outside, she knew the weather had worsened. The boat heaved from one side to the other, tipping nearly sideways at times, its hull groaning in protest.

She had to get out of there. Already the air was difficult to breathe, even with the open hatch nearby. She tested the rope at her wrist. Clint had tied only one of her arms, so if she could untie it with her other . . . but no. He'd cleverly placed the knot underneath the bunk, where she couldn't reach it.

She pulled in utter frustration. To her surprise, the wooden planks she was tied to split and broke apart, obviously rotten to the core. Another jerk, and she was free.

With the scrap of wood still hanging from her arm, Marissa climbed the stairs, took a deep breath of fresh air, then began making her way toward the back of the boat. It occurred to her then that the boat's engine had stopped. Lightning flashed overhead, and thunder boomed all around her. She gave up on the blanket, leaving it behind. At this point it was nothing but a dead, soggy weight.

When she reached the back of the boat, she looked up at the cockpit. No one was there. Then she saw the younger man leaning over the back of the boat. He shined a flashlight at something going on below. "You almost got it. It's moving."

She stepped up to the railing and peered into the murky depths. Clint was clamoring around on a huge tree. As wave after wave crashed over him, she couldn't imagine how he managed to hold on. She could see now that the tree was lodged in the boat's propeller.

The younger man glanced over at her, then did a

double take. "What are you doing up here?" He advanced toward her menacingly.

Instinctively, Marissa held up the piece of wood she was tied to and held it aloft like a club. "Don't you come near me."

He stopped, backed off. "Okay, chill out." He returned his attention to the goings-on in the water. "Hey, Clint, your hostage is running loose."

Clint seemed not to hear. He was doing battle with the tree trunk. At last, with a great shrieking of wood, the tree came loose—and so did Clint. He was flailing around, trying to keep his head above water, and the distance between him and the boat began to grow.

He waved his arms frantically.

"What are you doing?" Marissa demanded. "Throw him the rope!"

The man looked at her. "What do you care if he drowns?"

She wasn't sure exactly, but she knew she couldn't stand by and let it happen. Just because she'd been a kidnapping victim, she wouldn't lower herself to their standards. Without thinking, she grabbed the coil of rope and tossed it out to Clint while she held on to one end. Before the rope could get taut, she secured her end to the railing, tying the best Girl Scout square knot she could. The piece of wood dangling from her wrist hampered her somewhat, as did the boat's incessant pitching, but she still managed to get the job done.

When she was finished, she shielded her face from the rain with one hand and looked out, then gasped. Clint was fifty feet from the boat—but he had hold of the rope.

If he wasn't completely exhausted, he would be able to pull himself back to safety.

She turned to the other man, her illogical anger suddenly filling her, spilling over. "Nice move. What's the matter with you? He's the only one around here who knows anything about boats and navigation. Do you really want him to drown?"

The young man finger-combed his wet hair out of his face, then smiled. "I hadn't thought of that. You know, you're pretty smart for a girl."

What kind of troglodyte was this guy? It was futile to argue with his type. "Why don't you see if you can help your buddy back into the boat?" she suggested with no small amount of sarcasm. "Then you two can deal with the other problem."

"Yeah? What problem is that?"

"Something's on fire. The sleeping cabin is full of smoke."

She actually enjoyed the look of panic that wiped away the jerk's smug grin. He scampered over to where the rope was tied. "Clint?" he called. "Hurry. There's a fire!"

Marissa stood at the railing, watching with relief as Clint made steady progress toward the boat, hand over hand, inch by inch. Finally he reached the ladder. He clung there for a few moments, catching his breath, then began his ascent. It was Marissa who offered him a hand of support when he reached the railing. Clint's buddy stood there, apparently too confounded by recent events to be any help at all.

Clint came over the railing and fell to the deck in a

heap, dragging Marissa with him. Rather than try to pull away, she huddled there with him, unbearably relieved to feel the hardness of his body next to hers, real and secure. She'd been frightened for him. He could have drowned so easily. He was coughing up seawater.

"Are you okay?" she asked, alarmed.

He nodded, still coughing. "How'd you . . . get . . . loose?"

"Well, you ought to be glad I did, or you'd be fish food by now!" So much for her tender concern. "Your partner in crime is about as useful as a bicycle to a fish."

"Hey!" the younger man objected. "Don't listen to her. She threatened to club me to death with that hunk of wood. Can't you tie her up again?"

"Not now, not in this weather," Clint replied. "She may need to swim." He looked at her, really looked her in the eye for the first time since reboarding the vessel. "How come you're not wearing a life jacket?"

"Show me one."

"Rusty!" he bellowed, using his friend's name for the first time. "Get her a life jacket. If she drowns, we'll be guilty of capital murder, you know."

The man called Rusty was already donning his own life jacket, a sorry, withered little orange thing that resembled the one Clint had around his neck. "Nothing doing, man. There's only one life jacket left, and it's mine."

Clint swore, then took his own life jacket off and handed it to Marissa. "Put this on."

"But what about—"

"I'm a great swimmer, a world-class swimmer. I almost made the Olympic team in '76. Mark Spitz beat me out."

She let the lie pass, warmed by Clint's generosity. Maybe he'd rather drown himself than face a capital murder charge, but she suspected he was simply being a nice guy. There was something about him—something noble. She suspected that this act of terrorism was not his usual style. Something had driven him to it.

She found herself hoping that, for his sake, his lady friend, Rachelle, was somewhere safe and sound.

"There's a fire somewhere on board," she said almost matter-of-factly. This whole episode had taken on a surreal feel, as if it were a dream. "The sleeping cabin is all full of smoke."

"Aw, hell." He pushed himself to his feet, staggering as the boat lurched. "That stalled prop probably caused the engine to catch fire. Rusty, any fire extinguishers on board?"

Rusty shrugged.

"I saw one," Marissa said, remembering a red cylinder hanging on the wall in the cabin where she'd slept. "I'll go get it."

"Hurry," Clint said.

She went as fast as the pitching boat would let her, always keeping hold of something nailed down so she wouldn't get tossed overboard. At times the rain-slick deck was almost vertical. The cabin was thick with smoke by now, but there were no flames. The smoke was seeping in from somewhere else. Marissa held her breath and descended the stairs. At the bottom she turned to the right and felt along the wall until she found the red tank.

She pulled it from its moorings and dashed back up to the deck with it, praying the thing would work. Given the state of the rest of this scow, she had her doubts.

When she found Clint, he'd just opened another hatch, this one apparently to the engine room. A huge cloud of black smoke erupted from below, causing everyone to jump back, but the smoke cleared pretty quickly. Marissa handed Clint the extinguisher. He switched on a flashlight and entered the hatch. Marissa still didn't see any flames.

Clint reemerged a few moments later. "Well, the good news is, the fire appears to be out."

"Oh, thank God," Marissa said. Rusty issued a similar response.

"The bad news is, before it went out, the fire burned a big ol' hole through the hull. We're taking on water faster than we could ever bail it out."

"What, exactly, does that mean?" Rusty asked, his voice laced with panic.

Marissa already knew. "We're sinking, you dolt!"

FOUR

In all his years, Clint had never seen an operation go so badly. From the moment he discovered Marissa pointing that gun at him, nothing had worked out as expected. He had a strong inclination to bag the whole thing.

Then he thought of Rachelle. Frightened. Injured. Tortured. Dead. No matter what she'd done, she didn't deserve such a fate. Right now, Clint was her only hope. He had to save this operation, that was all there was to it. His first order of business was getting his hostage safely to shore.

"Put on that life jacket," he told Marissa. The shriveled orange thing was still dangling from her hand. "How did you get loose, anyway?"

"The wood was rotten," she said, hollering to be heard over the wind and rain. "Good thing, too, or I might have choked to death from the smoke while you were floating out to sea."

God, she was right. She'd thrown the rope to him,

and she'd alerted him to the fire, which could easily have caused an explosion, killing them all. He'd thank her later. Right now, he needed to make preparations. The wind was blowing the *Phen-Hu* toward land. They would probably land somewhere along the western shore of Trinity Bay, if the boat didn't swamp before then. That was a big *if*.

When Marissa continued to hold the life jacket, Clint snatched it from her and put it around her neck. Two of the three fastenings broke when he tried to hook them together. When he finished with the life jacket, he untied her wrist from the rotten wood plank and threw the whole mess overboard. All the while he worked, excruciatingly aware of her nearness and the way her skin felt against his fingertips, she looked up at him belligerently. The combination of fear, anger, and condemnation in her eyes almost undid him. No woman had ever looked at him that way before.

"What do we do now?" Rusty didn't sound at all happy. That cocksure composure had deserted him.

"We'll wait it out," Clint answered, trying not to sound as worried as he felt. He didn't want to have to deal with anyone's hysteria. Right now, Rusty was the most likely one to lose control. Marissa was taking everything stoically. "I'll get our things ready, in case we have to bail out." He made sure Marissa was holding on to something solid before he left her to her own devices.

Inside the hold he found the supplies Rusty had brought, packed in a waterproof bag—some bread and cheese, a couple of apples, a pair of handcuffs, a wad of cash, and an extra change of clothing for each of them, though nothing for Marissa. He threw the cellular phone in with everything else, then paused. What was that thunk, when the phone landed?

He fished around in the bag and came up with a gun. "Dammit, Rusty . . ." Clint had told Rusty at least ten times, *no guns.* He was tempted to throw it overboard, but he'd never hear the end of it if he did. Hell, the damn thing was loaded too. Clint emptied out the bullets, then repacked the weapon.

He foraged for a few more supplies from the *Phen-Hu*—a flashlight, a flare in case they were forced to SOS for help, and a small coil of rope. He felt bad for the family who owned this old heap. He hoped it was insured against theft.

He zipped the bag closed. Since it was water-resistant, it would probably make a good flotation device. Just the same, Clint wrapped it in a couple of trash bags he'd found in the hold and tied the ends with multiple knots.

By the time he returned to the deck, the rain had let up. So had the lightning and thunder. The boat was listing heavily to starboard, though. Clint figured she had less than an hour before she met her end. He wished he hadn't left his wet suit behind.

Marissa had found a handhold along the port railing and was clinging to it gamely. "What now, Ace?" she asked when she saw Clint approaching with his trash-bag-wrapped parcel.

"You know," Rusty put in, "you got a sharp mouth, lady. You oughtta be glad we didn't just slit your throat and—"

"That's enough!" Clint barked. "For God's sake,

Rusty, this isn't her fault." He turned to Marissa. "Nobody is slitting anybody's throat, okay?"

Rusty gave his signature giggle. "You're lousy as a kidnapper, man," he said. "You're supposed to keep your victim intimidated. Once we get to shore, what's to stop her from screaming her lungs out for help?"

"I didn't say I wouldn't gag her," Clint said with a shrug. He found his own handhold and grabbed it, keeping a tight grip on the trash-bag bundle with the other hand. "Nothing to do but wait it out for a while. When it's time to swim, I want everyone to head for the midpoint between those two lights."

Marissa nodded, but then she scanned the faraway shoreline. Clint wondered if she was contemplating how to make her escape. If she was going to do it, this would be the best time.

For a while, they were all quiet, listening to the *Phen-Hu*'s groaning death throes.

The boat gave a loud creak and a violent lurch. Marissa screamed—she couldn't help herself. As awful as the old fishing vessel had been, it was still better than letting that cold, black water claim her.

How much longer did they have? she wondered. They'd been drifting maybe an hour, and the shore didn't seem any closer at all. She wasn't a great swimmer, and the smelly orange thing around her neck hardly seemed capable of helping to keep her afloat.

She was cold. The rain had let up a while ago, but she was soaked through and through, and the wind chilled her to the bone. She'd started shivering, and now the tremors were uncontrollable.

"You cold?" Clint asked.

Well, duh. Who wouldn't be? But she couldn't even summon the oomph for a smart comeback. She nodded miserably instead.

"What happened to your blanket?"

"It's no use," she said. "The blanket is sopping wet. It's in the sleeping cabin if you want it."

"I thought you might. It might block the wind."

She shook her head. "We'll be swimming pretty soon, anyway, right?"

"Yeah." He looked up at the sky, then cupped his ear with his hand. "Sooner than I thought. Sounds like the Coast Guard put a chopper up. They'll be looking for vessels in trouble. When they find this one, we'd better not be on it."

That gave Marissa a brilliant idea. "Coast Guard," she said brightly as she, too, heard the distinctive sound of a helicopter. Maybe she could be rescued! Her arm was starting to ache from clinging to the handhold and trying to stick to the almost vertical deck.

"If that's the Coast Guard, I'm outta here," Rusty said as he held on to the boat with one hand and peeled his jeans off with the other. "I'll take my chances in the water. See y'all on shore."

"Rusty, wait—" But he'd already made his leap into the water. Clint stared after his coconspirator as he bobbed up and down on the waves, more or less swimming with a thrashing motion.

Clint shook his head. "Hell, no wonder he wanted a life jacket," he muttered.

The boat made another great heave. The water around them boiled up in bubbles.

"She's a goner," Clint said. "We better go. You ready?"

Marissa nodded. "You go first. I'd rather have a target to jump for." It was only a few feet to the waterline now, but Clint, thank goodness, bought her explanation.

"Okay. Jump right after me. I don't want us to get separated." He threw his bundle into the water, then dived in after it. Immediately he surfaced, clinging to the buoyant black trash bags. "Come on, Marissa."

"No!" she called. "I'm waiting here for the Coast Guard. You go ahead."

Clearly he hadn't been prepared for her mutiny. "What, are you crazy? In the first place, what if it's not the Coast Guard?" he called back to her. "You'll drown out here by yourself."

"I'll take my chances! You better start swimming, Ace. Your partner's getting ahead of you!"

"No, I'll wait for you," he said, sounding almost patient.

Damn, why didn't he save his own skin? Was he really worried about her, or was he trying to preserve his hostage, his leverage?

In the end, the decision to go or wait was taken out of her hands. The *Phen-Hu* gave a mighty shudder, then began a violent descent. With a scream Marissa abandoned ship. She hit the surface with a hard splash that nearly broke her neck. The water swallowed her, but then she bobbed up, coughing.

Clint was beside her in an instant. "You okay?"

"I've . . . been . . . better," she said between coughs. "Let's just start . . . swimming, okay?" Maybe the forced activity would warm her up. She felt like a human ice cube.

After the first few minutes, she and Clint got into a rhythm, each of them holding on to one side of their trash-bag buoy. She knew he could probably swim twice as fast without dragging her along, but he didn't abandon her, for which she was pathetically, though silently, grateful.

Soon her strength began to lag. With each wave that washed over them, she found it a little more difficult to hold her breath, then fight her way to the surface. Several times she inhaled a bunch of water, then spent valuable time and energy coughing it up.

If only she weren't so numbingly cold! Pretty soon, it felt as if she were trying to drag her arms and legs through gelatin instead of plain water. The shore appeared closer, then receded like in a bad dream. When she closed her eyes—it felt so good—pinpoints of light exploded behind her eyelids.

"Marissa? You okay?"

Clint had been asking her the same question every few minutes. Each time, she'd gamely answered that she was hanging in there. This time, she remained silent.

"Marissa!"

"I'm not all right!" she objected. "I'd rather drown

than swim one more yard!" Her arms and legs were burning on the inside while freezing on the outside.

Clint immediately stopped. Gratefully, she let her body go limp. The inadequate life jacket barely held her head above the water.

"Why didn't you tell me you were in trouble?"

She didn't answer. She didn't have the energy. At least the water wasn't as rough. Maybe that meant they were getting close to shore.

"Just lie back," he said, his voice surprisingly gentle. "I'll tow you the rest of the way. It's not much farther."

She closed her eyes and put her life into his hands.

Guilt ate at the edges of Clint's consciousness even as he struggled for survival. Marissa wasn't simply tired. She was suffering from hypothermia, if his guess was correct. Thank God the shore was looming closer.

Dawn was breaking. The storm was well over with, and Clint could now see that they were heading for a nice, convenient expanse of uninhabited, muddy beach.

No, not uninhabited. A lone figure waited for them. Apparently Rusty had made it alive. Clint had been so worried about his and Marissa's survival, he'd spared Rusty only a few moments of worry.

Clint's feet touched bottom. He savored the support for all of five seconds, then began laboriously dragging himself, Marissa, and his water-logged bundle of supplies to dry land.

"What took y'all so long?" Rusty asked. It hadn't

taken long for his cockiness to return, even while pacing the shore in his underwear.

"We have to move fast," Clint said without preamble, pitching his bundle onto shore, then lifting Marissa into his arms. She was conscious, but he didn't know how long she'd remain that way. "We need to find the nearest house and call an ambulance."

"Ambulance?" Marissa said between shivering teeth and lips that were tinged with blue.

"How about a motel?" Rusty asked, sounding not very concerned about their hostage. "I already reconnoitered a little bit, while it was still dark. There's a highway right over there, and a cheap motel not a quarter mile away."

Maybe Rusty had some redeeming value after all. "Good. That'll do." They could put Marissa in a hot shower. If she didn't show immediate improvement, Clint would give in and call the paramedics. It was better to face jail than to have this lovely woman's death on his conscience.

If he had this to do over again, he thought with chagrin as he and Rusty quickly donned their dry clothes . . . well, he wouldn't do it over again.

Clint kept his own soggy T-shirt, then quickly stripped Marissa of hers and put her into the remaining dry one from the waterproof bag. As he picked her up and followed Rusty toward the motel, he tried not to think about the glimpse of her creamy, rose-tipped breasts he'd gotten during the shirt-changing business.

Sure enough, the Riviera Motel, which advertised water beds, air conditioning, and color TV, was squatting right beside the two-lane shore road, less than a football field away. The vacancy sign blinked, although both *C*'s were burned out.

As they approached, Clint paused and handed Rusty a couple of bills from the wad he'd stuck in his pocket. "You go in and get us a double room. I'll wait with Marissa behind that van until I see you come out with the key."

Rusty raised his eyebrows. "A double room? All three of us? Who gets to share a bed?"

"Just do it, okay?" Clint would worry about sleeping arrangements later. Right now, all he could think about was getting Marissa warm.

With a shrug, Rusty took off at a lope toward the motel's office. Ah, youth, Clint thought. He knew Rusty wasn't in great physical shape—he never worked out. But he still had energy to spare after that grueling swim. Clint was dead on his feet.

He hated being forty.

He set Marissa down on the hood of an Oldsmobile. She was drowsy, but she opened her eyes when he said her name. "How do you feel?"

"Sleepy," she said. She was still shivering, dammit. But at least she had some color in her cheeks.

He put his arms around her, hoping to transfer some of his rapidly returning body heat to her. Her skin was cool to the touch, but not icy. Clint suddenly had all kinds of ideas for warming it up, but he quickly put a lid on such thoughts. He meant what he'd told Gabriole— his sister was a tempting package, especially when she rested her head on his shoulder as if she were a trusting kitten. But she was one temptation Clint wouldn't give in to.

Rusty emerged from the office five minutes later holding a key aloft. Clint picked up Marissa as well as the bag of supplies and followed. His arms and legs were burning by the time he reached the room. Rusty collapsed onto one of the beds. Clint headed for the bathroom. He leaned Marissa into a corner of the shower stall—there wasn't a tub—stripped the dry shirt off her, and fiddled with the faucets until he had a stream of comfortably warm water going. Then he stood her underneath it.

She wasn't very happy about that. She sputtered and cursed for a few seconds until she seemed to realize how good the warm water felt. Then she stood compliantly, letting the water sluice over her hair, her clothes, and down her bare legs. She probably had no idea what a fetching picture she presented. It was all Clint could do not to shuck his clothes and jump in with her.

She was more than sleepy or exhausted, he realized. She really was suffering from hypothermia. If she didn't perk up real soon, he would have to call an ambulance. He and Rusty could leave after making the 911 call. But once Marissa found her voice, Clint figured his odds of escaping this mess with no one the wiser were nil to zero. She knew his name was Clint, and she knew he was FBI. One phone call was all it would take.

Fortunately, Clint was saved from having to make that decision. Marissa rejoined the land of the living after about five minutes in the hot shower. She looked up at Clint and blinked confusedly. "Did I miss something?"

"I don't know. What's the last thing you remember?" Clint asked with a deliberate lack of concern in his voice. Inwardly he was jumping up and down over her improvement.

"We were swimming . . . I guess we didn't drown. Did I fall asleep or something?"

"Or something."

"Where are we?"

"At a motel." Clint turned off the shower faucet and handed her a towel. She was standing on her own now, only a little wobbly. "I'll give you some privacy," he said, glancing at the bathroom's only window. It was tiny and looked thoroughly closed. He decided not to worry. "Get out of those wet clothes and dry yourself off. There's a bed in the next room with your name on it."

"That sounds like heaven—wait a minute. If I take off my clothes, what do I put on?"

He shrugged. "I don't have any extra clothes for you. We'll have to dry yours off. Meanwhile, just wrap up in a towel and hop under the covers. Rusty's already asleep, and I won't look." Yeah, right.

Marissa didn't believe him any more than he believed himself, if her skeptical look was any indication. But she finally agreed. "Okay, fine." She grabbed the towel and attacked her hair with it. "I'll be out in a minute."

Clint hightailed it out of that bathroom before he could even think about touching her again. Marissa, complacent and trusting, was a turn-on, but when she went all feisty on him, she really did things to his libido.

Marissa actually smiled as soon as Clint closed the bathroom door. She was on dry land, and she was almost warm! She felt in a much stronger position. If she managed to escape, she could actually run out into the street rather than into the water.

She immediately checked the window, but that route was useless. The tiny opening was covered with frosted glass and some kind of anti-break-in wire mesh, then bolted shut like Fort Knox.

As she shimmied out of her wet clothes and hung them over the shower rod, Marissa began to formulate a plan. Clint was obviously concerned about her—perhaps more worried about her welfare than her escape potential. She'd been groggy and confused a few minutes earlier. She would continue to act that way. Maybe Clint would forget to tie her up, as he'd done when she was seasick.

When she was reasonably dry she wrapped the threadbare beige towel around her as modestly as possible, then sat down on the floor to wait. She closed her eyes, thinking she could easily drift off, making her act all the more believable.

Clint didn't give her that luxury. "Marissa?" he called through the bathroom door. "You okay in there?"

"Mmph?" she answered.

He came right on in and picked her up as if she were a doll. Her towel was gaping, but to tug at it would give away her true state of alertness.

Clint's face, though, was etched with concern, not lust, and she felt a twinge of guilt over misleading him. "C'mon, darlin'," he said, "let's get you warm." He carried her out of the bathroom and over to the bed. The room was warm. It felt great. He laid her gently onto the sheets and stretched the blankets up to her neck. She glanced over at the other bed. Rusty was passed out. He hadn't even bothered to take off his shoes.

She thought her plan had worked until Clint quickly, efficiently, reached under the covers and grabbed her right arm, the one closest to the edge of the bed. He pulled it out and efficiently cuffed her to the bed frame with a murmured "sorry."

Not half as sorry as she was, she thought, fuming. Clint might be a lot of things, but stupid wasn't one of them. She had one defense left, and that was screaming. Maybe someone in a nearby room would hear and come to investigate. One thing was certain. She wasn't going to lie there passively, waiting for something else horrible to happen.

Without warning, she opened her mouth and gave a blood-freezing scream. "Help! Help, I've been kid—"

Clint was on her in an instant. He hadn't merely put his hand over her mouth, he'd practically tackled her. Now not only did she have a large hand half smothering her, but she was being crushed by two hundred pounds of pure male muscle.

It really wasn't so bad, having Clint lying on top of her. A series of pictures flashed through her mind, X-rated images of a few other scenarios involving a similar proximity of bodies, hers and Clint's. Egad, where had *that* come from?

She'd stopped screaming the instant Clint made his move. Now she was utterly silent, except for her heart, which was thumping like the march of a very determined soldier.

"What the hell—" Rusty was off the bed, looking around, confused.

"Nothing, Rusty," Clint said calmly. "Just our little hostage, playing games. Making me believe she was sick. Making me *worry* about her."

"Mfmpf," she said.

"Not a chance. I don't want to hear a word you have to say." He turned back to Rusty. "Find me something to gag her with, will you?"

"You don't have to gag her," Rusty said. "I don't think there's anybody else staying at this motel. It's like a ghost town."

That damn Rusty, Marissa thought. For once, he had to be smart. Her screaming had accomplished nothing except to sentence her to a gag.

"Just find me a sock or something."

Before she knew what was happening, Clint was holding a pair of socks over her mouth and was tying them tight with a strip from a torn pillowcase.

"I hate doing this, you know," he said. "But I can't have you calling for help, not now. This won't last much longer, I promise."

Yeah, right. He'd said it would be over before morning. She didn't know what time it was, but judging from the sunlight filtering in through the drawn curtains, it was morning.

"Try to get some sleep, will you?"

Easy for him to say. He didn't have a pair of socks blocking his mouth. She closed her eyes anyway. Clint sat down on the end of her bed. She felt the mattress give. He must be at least as tired as she was. Would he become more desperate as exhaustion settled in?

"We need to call Gabriole again," he announced to Rusty. "Ol' Jimmy's had plenty of time to think about his situation."

And to call the police, Marissa hoped as she cracked her eyes open to watch. She dreaded the thought of Jimmy trying to handle this on his own or, God forbid, with the help of his friends. Much as she wanted to be free, she couldn't stand the thought of bloodshed on her behalf. If Jimmy would be patient, Clint would tire of this game and let her go. She was sure of that. He wouldn't do the things he'd threatened to do with her.

Clint stood, almost reluctantly it seemed, and reached into his bag for the cellular phone. He raised the antenna, punched in a few numbers, then cursed. "Damn, what else could go wrong?"

"What?" Rusty asked.

"The battery's dead. I put a fresh one in right before I gave the phone to you. What'd you do, call Australia?"

Clint had apparently guessed right, and Rusty, the idiot, was too dumb to lie his way out of it. "I might have made a few calls. Hell, it was free, and you said it was untraceable. I haven't called my mom in almost two months, since they disconnected my phone, so I thought—"

"Never mind. Now I'll have to find a public phone someplace, and hope to hell Jimmy hasn't gone to the cops, that he's not tracing the call."

"Even if he is, you can get away from the phone booth

in plenty of time to avoid being nabbed," Rusty pointed out.

"Yeah," Clint reluctantly agreed. "But it's not the way I planned on handling this thing."

"So? Why's that different than anything else about this job?" Rusty laughed. The sound sent shivers right to Marissa's bones.

"You got a point. I'll be gone maybe half an hour, if all goes well. Just keep an eye on her." He nodded toward Marissa. "Make sure she doesn't get loose. Make sure she's breathing. And for God's sake, don't touch her otherwise. Leave her alone."

"You got it, boss," Rusty said with a mock salute.

Looking not very reassured, Clint left the motel room.

Marissa immediately felt more uneasy, if that was possible. She definitely did not like being left alone with Rusty the Giggle Man. He was a couple of bricks short of a load.

Rusty watched out a crack in the curtain for several tense seconds. Then he turned toward Marissa. "Man, I thought he'd never leave. Are you okay? Jimmy the Gab would never forgive me if I let anything happen to you. Sorry I had to talk so rough to you earlier. That was just an act to convince Clint."

Jimmy the *what*?

"Ah, I see you don't quite get it yet, do you? I'm on your side, sweet cakes. This is all a setup. Clint's precious Rachelle is alive and well, probably lying in Eddie's bed and snorting coke this very minute. I talked to her last night. She said her job was to flush Clint out and force him into a desperate move. And now I'm gonna nail him. If this doesn't earn me a top spot in the organization, I don't know what will."

Marissa's head swam. Rusty worked for Eddie Constantine? Rachelle hadn't really disappeared? And what exactly did Rusty mean by "nail him"?

"Man, listen to me, blathering on and leaving you all trussed up. Here, let's get that gag off of you. You're okay, right? You won't scream no more or nothing, right? 'Cause I'm on your side. As soon as I finish my business here, we'll go call Eddie and Jimmy, or anyone else you want, and you can go home. This nightmare will be over."

She felt a momentary burst of relief at having the gag removed. And the thought of calling Jimmy, of telling him she was safe . . . But what was this "business" of Rusty's?

She licked her lips. Her best bet was to play along until she could figure out what was going on and formulate another plan. "Thanks," she said, rubbing her face with her free hand. "What about the handcuffs?"

"Oh, uh, I'm afraid Clint must have taken the key with him. But we'll get it soon as he comes back. You know, I tried to get rid of him on the boat. Why'd you go and throw him the rope? Sure would have been cleaner if he'd drowned."

Marissa stifled a gasp. She was beginning to get the picture, and it was an ugly one. "Clint was the only one among us who could navigate," Marissa said. "Unless you were hiding some sailing skills."

"Hah, not that that mattered in the end. It's okay,

though. He might have survived, if we'd let him drift away from the boat. A bullet in the brain, though, that's a sure thing." He giggled.

Marissa felt herself going dizzy. He talked about cold-blooded murder as casually as if he were discussing fixing a leaky gasket on his car.

Rusty went to the zippered case and dug around inside. "Yeah, I knew ol' Clint wouldn't be able to leave my piece behind." He pulled out a gun—a big, black revolver—then checked the cylinder. "Damn, he unloaded it."

Marissa's hopes soared until she realized Rusty had found the bullets. He pushed them into the cylinder one by one, then snapped the gun closed. "Ready for takeoff."

Marissa felt as if she might throw up. Obviously Rusty assumed that both she and Jimmy operated in the same sick world as Eddie and Rachelle and himself—and Clint, for that matter.

"What about the motel clerk?" Marissa asked. "After they find Clint's b-body . . ." She faltered a bit on that word. ". . . won't he or she be able to identify you?"

"Nah. When I went in, no one was behind the front desk, so I just liberated a key. No one saw a thing."

This guy was serious. He was going to kill Clint in cold blood—and, she realized with a start, she was the only person who could prevent it.

FIVE

Rusty reclaimed his bed, lying on top of the covers, his head propped up by two pillows, his feet crossed negligently at the ankles. He had the gun in his hand, resting against his stomach.

"I'm gonna get some more sleep. You holler if you hear the man coming, okay?"

"Yeah, sure. I can't sleep, anyway." Marissa tried to sound nonchalant, though her heart was racing. Maybe Rusty would be asleep when Clint returned, and she could warn Clint—no, that wouldn't work. Rusty had the only room key. She'd seen him pocket it after opening the door. Clint would have to knock to get into the room.

She had to either get to the phone, get to the gun—or disable Rusty. Her third option was the most distasteful, but unfortunately the most likely to meet with success. The phone was across the room, well out of her reach; any attempt she made to take the gun might result in his waking and shooting her. At any rate, he would know they weren't on the same side.

So she had to disable him. And try not to kill him in the process.

She waited until she heard him softly snoring, then began experimenting. She had little mobility with her hand cuffed to the metal bed frame. But she could maneuver herself out of bed, and she had one free hand and two free feet to work with. However, there were a limited number of things she could reach—pillows and blankets, a telephone book, a lamp.

A lamp. As a weapon it lacked subtlety, but it would have to do. She reached behind the nightstand as quietly as possible and unplugged the lamp. It was a heavy ceramic number, with cacti and sunburst patterns on it.

She took off the shade, then hefted the base experimentally with her left arm. She didn't have much control. But if she grabbed the lamp by the harp, with the bottom part over her head, then all she would need to do was lean it in the right direction. Gravity would do a lot of the work.

She couldn't believe it. She, Marissa Gabriole, who had deplored and shunned violence for the last twenty years, was about to bash in a man's head—while he was sleeping and defenseless. Well, not quite defenseless, she reasoned. There was the gun.

She had no choice, she reminded herself. She was saving Clint's life—whether it deserved saving or not. She didn't need to kill Rusty, just stun him long enough to allow her to get that gun away. She would have to *keep* the gun under her control too. It shamed her to remember how easily Clint had disarmed her.

The longer she delayed, the worse her chances of success got. Rusty could wake up any time. Clint could return. She gritted her teeth, begged God's forgiveness, and with all her strength heaved the lamp at Rusty's head.

The lamp shattered. Rusty made a surprised grunt, then fell silent. Marissa grabbed the gun, then jumped back, ready for anything. She pointed the revolver toward Rusty's limp form. Nothing. Oh, dear God, what if she'd killed him?

She stuck the gun under her pillow and began pulling pieces of the lamp away from Rusty's face. A trickle of blood stained his forehead, but he looked otherwise intact, and he was breathing.

She'd just released her own pent-up breath when a knock sounded on the door. "Rusty, it's me. Open up!"

Clint! What was she going to tell him? He'd probably never believe her story. "Clint?" she called to him. "You'll have to break the door. Rusty's unconscious, and I can't reach the lock."

"What?" Rusty unconscious? Just when Clint was beginning to think he was making progress. He felt the first stirrings of panic. Was Rusty having some delayed reaction to the previous night's trauma? Had he hit his head? Was he merely exhausted?

Without further delay, Clint placed a series of well-aimed kicks to the door. The cheap particleboard gave way as if it were balsa wood. He burst into the room . . .

and for the second time in twenty-four hours, he came upon Marissa Gabriole holding a gun pointed at him.

"That's far enough," she said. "Don't think I'll be stupid enough to surrender a gun to you a second time. If I'd had any idea what you were planning to put me through, I'd have shot you when I first laid eyes on you."

"What the hell happened?" was all Clint could think of to ask. Man, he leaves for fifteen minutes, and all hell breaks loose.

"I saved your miserable life, that's what happened," she said, confusing him even further. "You've got the handcuff key. Toss it over here."

He wasn't about to. In her current state, she couldn't chase him if he resorted to fleeing. "First, explain how it is you think you saved my life."

"It's your so-called partner," she said, nodding toward Rusty. "Apparently Eddie Constantine is tired of you picking on him, and he wants you dead. Rusty was planning to earn some brownie points by doing the deed."

This made no sense at all. "And leave his sister spinning in the wind? I don't think so."

"His sister—Rachelle, right?"

Clint nodded.

"He says Rachelle is safe. Her disappearance was a setup to flush you out. You're getting too close to something. I think Rachelle must have told Rusty about it last night, when they talked."

Clint rolled his eyes, though Marissa's words made him feel distinctly uneasy. "Why would I believe a cockamamy story like that?"

"That's why he took out the gun," she said, sounding a little desperate. "He was lying on the bed, waiting for you, and he fell asleep. I had to do something—I couldn't let him shoot you down in cold blood. So I hit him with the lamp."

"Why not let him kill me?" Clint asked, sounding a lot more confident than he felt. He inched closer to her. "You're ready to do it yourself, right? That's what you were saying."

Panic registered in her dark eyes. She wiggled the gun. "I will too. You stop right there. Don't you come any closer!"

He took another step.

She pulled the trigger. The explosion of sound was deafening.

"Jeez Louise!" Clint did a fast-forward tap dance before he realized she'd missed. The bullet had landed behind him somewhere. "Okay, I'm staying way back, all right?"

But she wasn't listening to him. She was staring at the gun in her left hand. "Oh, my God, what have I done?" She dropped the gun onto the bed as if it were a snake. "Take it, just take the damn thing. Shoot me, I don't care."

Relief coursed through Clint's body, followed quickly by sympathy as he saw the stricken look on Marissa's face. He'd driven her to this, just as Gabriole had driven Clint to kidnapping and hijacking.

Hardening his heart against her, he stepped forward and took the gun. It was warm. He quickly emptied it of its remaining cartridges, threw it into his bag, then stepped into the bathroom and one by one dropped the bullets into the open sink drain. He should have thrown the gun overboard when he had the chance.

When he returned to the room, he found Marissa sitting on the edge of the bed, crying softly. The sound of her tears dug at his hard heart. He couldn't help himself. He sat down next to her and put an arm around her shoulders, trying not to notice how bare they were. That scanty towel was the only thing covering Marissa's favors. One good tug—

He closed his mind to that.

"It'll be okay, Marissa," he said. "Things are looking up. This'll all be over in a couple of hours. I spoke to your brother, and we're working things out."

She shook off his arm, scooted away from him. "Your partner is half dead over there. How can you say things are looking up?"

Hell, he'd almost forgotten about poor Rusty in all the confusion. He went over to the bed, checked the young man's pulse, his breathing. He lifted the eyelids. Both pupils contracted to the light. There was blood on his forehead from a small cut there, and a raised lump, but it didn't appear as if anything was broken.

"He's out cold, all right. You did this to him?" His admiration for her inched up another notch. She was one gutsy lady.

"You make me sick!" Marissa cried. "You claim to be trying to help your friend, who's disappeared. You have contempt for my brother because you think he did something to this . . . Rachelle. Well, my brother is ten times the man you are, Clint whatever-your-name-is. He might not always be inside the strict limits of the law, but he doesn't go around abducting people. He respects women."

"Is that so?" Clint couldn't help smiling at her naïveté. "Is that why he owns a strip club?"

"What are you talking about? He doesn't own any strip club."

Clint went into the bathroom to get a cold washcloth. When he returned to the room, he asked, "What do you call the Foxhunt?" He placed the cool, wet rag on Rusty's forehead. Rusty stirred and mumbled something.

"It's a—it's a restaurant," Marissa said, though she didn't sound very sure of herself. "I did a Schedule C for the Foxhunt."

"But have you ever been there?" He looked over his shoulder at her.

She shook her head, not meeting his gaze.

"You might be able to order food there, but the waitresses are all topless."

Marissa opened her mouth, then clamped it closed before finally coming up with a retort. "He didn't actually own it, you know," she said, her chin jutting out defensively. "On paper he did. But it really belongs to his friend, Eddie Constantine. Eddie's going through a divorce, and his wife is grabbing up assets as fast as she can, so Eddie talked Jimmy into being the front man for the Foxhunt so the lawyers wouldn't be able to take it away."

Interesting, Clint thought. This was something he hadn't known about. "Whether he owns it or not, he's sure as hell there every night, glad-handing, passing out free drinks to his best customers. I hear he particularly likes interviewing potential employees, if you get my drift. In fact, I think his current wife used to work for him."

"Who, Sophia?" Marissa's momentary confusion was replaced with sudden anger. "Oh, just stop it. You aren't going to convince me Jimmy is something he's not by telling a bunch of lies. Anyway, even if you believe what you're saying, even if you believe he's slime, are you any better? You're just another one of *them*, resorting to violence to get what you want."

"Hey, you're the one who tried to shoot me! It wasn't my idea to involve guns."

"I wasn't trying," she muttered. "I missed on purpose. Anyway, I suppose I'm no better than you, although at least I can claim self-defense."

Now Clint was the one at a loss for words. She was right. No matter how many times he kept telling himself that he was doing this for all the right reasons, he was behaving in a reprehensible fashion. If Marissa were his sister and someone did this to her—scared her to pieces, manhandled her, almost drowned her—he'd beat them to a pulp.

But Marissa wasn't his sister. In fact, he was feeling distinctly unbrotherly things toward her. Rather than use her as a pawn in his deadly game, he wanted to protect her. But how could you protect someone who'd been born into such a family? Daughter of Lido Gabriole and sister to Jimmy the Gab. Her own parents had been brutally murdered. There was little she could do to keep crime totally out of her life, even if she wanted to.

"You should move away," he murmured.

"What?"

"Never mind. Rusty's not responding. I think we better get him to a hospital." He went into the bathroom one more time. Marissa's clothes were still damp, but they would have to do. He came out and tossed them to her. "Put these on. I'll call nine-one-one, and then you and I will hightail it out of here before the ambulance arrives." Funny, but only a few minutes earlier he'd contemplated this exact plan of action, except that Marissa had been the one in need of medical care, and he'd visualized fleeing the scene with Rusty.

"Aren't you forgetting something?" She rattled the handcuffs.

"Right." Feeling a now-familiar tightness in his gut at having to go near her, he freed Marissa, though he intended to keep a close eye on her. He watched with disguised interest as she pulled the red T-shirt over her head, then shimmied into pink panties and the paisley boxer shorts, all without removing the towel until the very end. Damn, she was a looker, even in that crazy outfit.

He dialed 911, then left the phone off the hook without speaking to the operator. They'd trace the call and send someone. "Okay, let's go."

Subdued now, she went with him obediently, stepping gingerly in her bare feet through the debris that had once been their motel room door. "Where are we going?"

"We're going to borrow a car."

"Steal a car? Why am I not surprised? Last night you stole one boat and sank another one. A car should be no problem."

"It isn't." He'd already picked it out—a four-year-old Oldsmobile, sitting in the motel parking lot with the keys in the ignition. What was another five to ten years for auto theft added to his sentence? What mattered was that a few minutes before, Jimmy Gabriole had told him that Rachelle was alive. In a matter of hours, they would talk again and arrange for a transfer of hostages.

It was a few minutes later before Marissa felt she could even talk. What kind of person was she? She was beginning to wonder. She'd severely injured one man and almost shot another. Granted, in attacking Rusty she'd been trying to save Clint's life, but still.

"You don't seem to believe what I said before—that Rusty was going to kill you."

"It was a nice try, darlin', but no, I don't."

She really didn't blame him. Why would she have saved his life one minute, only to shoot at him the next? He had no way of knowing that her miss had been deliberate, intended to scare him. Even with her left hand, she could hit a six-foot-something man from eight feet away. Who couldn't?

"How do you explain the presence of the gun?" she asked. "It was stashed away and unloaded when you left."

"Rusty's a nut. He was probably pulling some macho number on you."

"And the gag? How did I remove it without Rusty's help?"

That one apparently stumped him.

"Clint, listen to me. You're being set up. Rusty didn't

tell me everything—he assumed I knew some things, that I'm in cahoots with Eddie simply because I'm Jimmy's sister. But I got the gist of it. You're involved in some FBI investigation, and you're getting too close to Eddie. Rachelle is a coke addict, and she'll do anything for a snort, even set you up to be killed."

She wasn't getting through to him, she could tell. And if she didn't, he might get them both killed.

"Listen to me!" she said again, hitting him in the arm.

"Ouch. Stop that."

"Well, listen, then. Remember when you were trying to fix the boat propeller, and you lost your grip? Do you remember that I was the one who threw you the rope? Rusty wasn't making any attempt to help you. He was going to let you drown. He told me that."

Clint glanced over at her. He didn't appear quite as sure of himself, but he said nothing.

"Clint, please, don't you get it? Eddie knew Rachelle was an informant. He paid her, or gave her drugs, to pull a number on you, to 'flush you out,' in Rusty's words."

"That can't be true," Clint said. "Rusty doesn't work for Eddie."

"Not yet, but he'd sure like to. He thought that killing you would be his ticket in."

Suddenly Clint pulled the car over to the shoulder and stopped. He turned and stared at Marissa, his face a reflection of his horror. "You aren't kidding about this."

Finally. He was going to believe her. She shook her head. "Much as I hate what you've done to me, I don't want you killed. I don't want anyone killed. God, what if Rusty dies and it's my fault?"

"Rusty isn't going to die. His vital signs were good—he just had a bump on the head. Now, I want you to tell me exactly what he told you, word for word, as nearly as you can remember."

Marissa went through her conversation with Rusty again. And then a second time. By the third recap, she could tell that Clint really did believe her. She could also see that he was deeply hurt by the possibility of Rachelle's betrayal.

"I still don't believe Rachelle could do this to me," he said, shaking his head. "We had our differences, we were married only a short time and our marriage was a disaster from start to finish, but there was some genuine fondness there. She saved my life once. She stepped in front of me and took a bullet. It almost killed her. How could she turn around and . . . ?" He couldn't even put it into words.

"Drugs," Marissa said. "She's an addict, according to Rusty."

Clint sighed deeply. "I've put her through detox more times than I can count. I thought she was gonna make it this time, although, in her profession, I guess she can't get away from it."

"Her profession? Your ex-wife is a . . ."

"Yeah. I married a stripper. Strange choice for an FBI agent, huh?"

To say the least. Marissa was having a hard time imagining it. Clint seemed so . . . straight, despite his recent crime spree. While he stared out the windshield, his mind no doubt a million miles away, she studied him. Square jaw, short, almost military-length hair—though a little longer on top, she noticed. Eyes a pale shade of blue—no they were gray, she decided. True gray. She'd never seen eyes that shade.

He was handsome in a tough-guy way, especially with that day's growth of beard. Her heart fluttered inside her chest. Did kidnap victims really fall in love with their captors? Was she turning into a modern-day Patty Hearst? Because, despite all that had happened, despite being kidnapped and hijacked and handcuffed by this man, she felt an almost irresistible urge to reach over and touch him. It was the pain she saw, so palpable she could feel it in her own gut, that made her want to give comfort.

She forced herself to resist. This situation was complicated enough.

Suddenly he looked at Marissa. "So what's Jimmy's role in all this?"

She closed her eyes, feeling her own wave of pain. That was the million-dollar question. "I don't know. I'd like to believe he's just a pawn, but—"

" 'But' is right. He's in up to his eyeballs."

"He wouldn't condone murder," she said with absolute certainty.

"A few minutes ago, you were convinced he couldn't own a strip club. But he does. I've seen him there with my own eyes. And his wife, Sophia, used to be a dancer. I know that for a fact."

Marissa sighed. "I can believe the strip club part. It's tough, but I can see it. But not murder. Anyway, if he was part of this conspiracy, wouldn't he have offered a bit more cooperation the first time you called?"

"Hmm, you have a point." He eased the car back into traffic on the two-lane blacktop.

"Isn't it possible that Eddie Constantine is setting up Jimmy too?" Marissa asked. "He had no way of knowing how you would react when you realized Rachelle was missing. What if you'd gone through proper channels instead of pulling the crazy stunt you did? Eddie wouldn't want his name connected to a missing person case. So Rachelle dropped hints that *Jimmy* was after her, that she was afraid of him, *not Eddie.*"

"Okay, that's one theory," Clint said. "If you like it better than mine, we'll go with it. For now."

"You mean the 'up-to-his-eyeballs' theory? Yeah, I like it better." Suddenly she was incredibly tired. She tipped her seat back and closed her eyes. "Where are we going, anyway?"

"We were heading for an FBI safe house in Pearland, but now I'm not so sure." His voice reflected bone weariness.

"You mean, the FBI's in on this kidnapping thing you did?" she asked.

"No. I'm on my own. I just know this one particular house is hardly ever used. It's kind of a dive. But I was thinking. . . . Hell, I oughtta let you go. Drop you near a pay phone. This operation was a bad idea from the very beginning. You know, I did go through the proper channels. And nobody gave a flip. My boss said that to go after Rachelle now would jeopardize the whole investigation." His knuckles whitened against the steering wheel. "He said she was nothing but a junkie stripper anyway, not worth the bother."

"Well, of course she's worth the bother," Marissa said hotly. "She's a human being, no matter what she's done wrong. And I'm sure you still care about her, the way I care about Jimmy no matter what he's gone and gotten himself mixed up in."

Clint said nothing. He simply kept driving.

"You'll really let me go?" she asked in a small voice.

"Yeah. Hell, I'm sorry, Marissa. For involving you, for almost getting you killed, for leaving you alone with Rusty so you ended up having to defend yourself against him—"

"I was defending you, not myself," she said succinctly. "Or don't you believe me still?"

He nodded. "I believe you. I guess I should thank you for saving my life."

"Twice," she reminded him. "I threw you the rope."

"And then you tried to shoot off my kneecaps."

"I told you, I missed on purpose."

"Yeah, with the gun in your left hand, shaking like a leaf. Do you have any idea what a ridiculous picture you made, half leaning, half sitting with one hand cuffed to the bed, the other holding that gun, that towel wrapped around you and about to fall off. . . ." His voice trailed off, and he went silent.

Marissa couldn't think of anything to say. Abruptly she changed the subject. "So, you talked to Jimmy?"

"Yeah. He said a friend of his knew something about Rachelle, and that he was willing to trade her for you. I'm supposed to call back at noon to find out how and where to make the trade."

"You see?" she said excitedly. "I'll bet they pick some deserted alley or pier. And they'll kill you."

"That's *not* going to be a happening thing. If Rachelle wasn't really kidnapped, there isn't much point in negotiating further." He paused, then asked, "Where do you want to be let off? I have three-quarters of a tank of gas. I'll take you anywhere in Houston you want to go."

It was on the tip of her tongue to tell him her home address. She would give anything to crawl into her own comfortable bed right then. She thought, *Am I crazy? Tell this deranged man where I live?* But she realized she wasn't afraid of Clint anymore.

He was really going to release her. Perversely, she wasn't quite ready to say good-bye. A crazy idea was forming in her brain. "Why don't we go to that safe house you mentioned?" she suggested. "We can talk, maybe get some sleep. Then, I've got a proposition for you."

SIX

Clint thought he was having an audio hallucination. "I said I'm letting you go. You're free. Don't you want to call the cops or something?"

"Maybe. Eventually. But I have an idea. I think you and I can help each other out—I can help with your investigation, and you . . ." She paused, looking pensive. "But I won't know for sure until I get some sleep and can think clearly again. So let's go to this safe house. Does it have beds?"

"Hell, yeah, it has beds," Clint said, stepping on the accelerator. He forced himself to slow down when he realized he was speeding. The last thing he needed right then was to be pulled over in a hot car. But he was feeling hopeful again. Apparently Marissa wasn't hell-bent on having him arrested, at least not yet. Maybe, just maybe, he wouldn't end up in the pen after all.

Before heading for the safe house, Clint decided to ditch the Olds and pick up his own wheels. His apartment was more or less on the way to the safe house. Marissa dozed in the passenger seat during the twenty-minute drive. He caught himself looking over at her as often as he could without driving off the road, wondering what in hell she had in mind. Why hadn't she left him when she had the chance? After everything he'd done. . . .

He parked in a convenience store lot close to his apartment complex just south of Hobby Airport. Marissa stirred.

"We're just changing cars, sweetheart," he said. When he realized the endearment had slipped out, he had to wonder where his own head was at. "Um, you're sure you don't want to . . ." He gestured. "I can handle this thing on my own, you know. It's not the first time some-one has wanted me dead."

"Typical male," she grumbled as she opened her door. "The Lone Ranger, always has to take care of things on his own. I'm not crazy about this situation. But now that I've gotten dragged into it, I don't feel right about walk-ing away—not if I can help you put some slime behind bars. What are you doing?"

"Wiping off fingerprints." He was using a tissue to clean every surface either one of them had touched— mirrors, seat belts, steering wheel. "I'm hoping if I leave the keys in it, someone else will steal it, and I'll be off the hook."

"Oh." Marissa grabbed another tissue from the travel box on the dash and began helping him. "You did say we're changing cars."

"My apartment's right around the corner." But he wanted to return to the former subject. "You want to help me put slime behind bars. So your angle in this is to do your part for society?"

"That's part of it, I guess. Look, I'm too tired to think this through right now. Don't go asking me hard questions, okay?"

He shrugged. "Okay." Truthfully, he was glad she was sticking around. He would miss her when she took off, despite her acerbic tongue. "You could be in danger, too, you know. If someone's after me, you could end up in the wrong place at the wrong time."

"I already was in the wrong place at the wrong time," she reminded him. "It couldn't get much worse than what I've already been through."

Clint didn't have a reply to that. Yeah, so he was scum. The plan had seemed sensible at the time.

They both got out of the Olds and started walking. Clint knew the rough blacktop couldn't feel good on Marissa's bare feet, but she didn't complain.

They cut down an alley and into a parking lot. His old 240Z was parked in a carport behind his generic-looking apartment building. He'd bought the Z the previous year and had been working nights and weekends ever since to return it to its former glory. Few people at the Bureau had even seen it; no one would think to look for it.

"Wow," Marissa said through a yawn. "Cool car."

"Thanks." Like a high-school hotshot, he took irrational pride in her compliment.

Back on the road, they were silent for a long time. Then Clint felt an odd urge to make small talk. He'd made all kinds of incorrect assumptions about Marissa Gabriole already. He wanted to know more about her.

"So, you're an accountant? Do you have your own practice?"

Marissa didn't answer. When he looked over at her, he realized she was asleep once more. No wonder, if she felt anywhere near as beat as he did. Sometimes, he just couldn't compensate for the fact that he was forty.

Thirty minutes later, they were pulling into the gravel driveway of an old white farmhouse in Pearland. Housing tracts had sprouted all around, but this house, and the twenty acres surrounding it, had resisted development. Actually, it was up for sale now. The Bureau had decided that, after fifteen years, it had outlived its usefulness as a safe house. Too many people knew about it, and too many neighbors had moved too close.

Clint found it perfect for his purposes. It wasn't air-conditioned, but this time of year that was okay. As he remembered it, the kitchen was June Cleaver–era, the furniture Early American Ugly. But if he ended up a wanted man, no one would think to look for him there, right in the Bureau's bosom, so to speak. He could only hope no one was planning to use it for an official purpose.

He shut off the car and loudly announced, "We're home!"

Marissa cracked one eye open. "This it?"

"Yup."

She yawned again. "Just lead me to a bed or a sofa or something."

"Coming right up." He got out, walked around, opened her door, and offered her a hand.

"Mmm, thanks. My muscles don't seem to be obeying me. All that swimming. . . ."

"You're probably gonna be some kind of sore in a few hours. I will too."

She took his hand, then, trustingly, unashamedly, leaned against him as they mounted the steps to the front porch. She was more asleep than awake, Clint reminded himself. She probably wasn't completely aware of what she was doing. Nonetheless, all that soft femininity so close to him was giving him fits.

Why did she have to smell so good, when he knew she'd put nothing on her skin except cheap-motel soap? She was dressed like a summertime vagrant, and her hair was tousled, yet she was the sexiest thing he'd ever seen. Or felt. Or smelled.

"How'd you get a key?" she asked when he unlocked the door.

So, she wasn't completely unaware. "Years ago I was in charge of guarding a witness out here. I lost the key, then found it again months later. I never bothered to return it. Figured it might come in handy someday—" He stopped.

"What? Oh . . ."

The living room was glaringly empty. Every stick of furniture had been moved out.

"So much for that bed you promised," Marissa huffed.

Clint dropped his bag and sprinted up the stairs. Maybe, by some miracle, something had been over-looked. But all three bedrooms were bare. Judging from the scent, the carpets had been recently cleaned too. The Bureau was probably spiffing the place up so they could unload it, and the hideous old furniture had no doubt been a liability.

He checked the linen cupboard. "Eureka."

"A bed?" Marissa asked hopefully. She'd followed him up the stairs.

"Pillows and blankets. Pick a bedroom and make yourself a pallet."

She frowned at him. "I'm tired enough to do just that." She grabbed an armload of linens and marched through the nearest door. Clint watched, amused, as she arranged things to her satisfaction, then flopped down on the floor. But a moment later, his amusement dimmed, replaced by something much more like lust. His whole body cried out to be near her, to lie down next to her.

He couldn't, though. He still had some business to take care of.

Marissa awoke with an unsettled feeling. Something wasn't right. She knew immediately where she was, but for the first time in hours she was alone. The house was eerily quiet.

She didn't think she'd slept long, maybe an hour, but it was enough for her brain to start working again. She stumbled into the bathroom and stared at her reflection in the mirror.

"Egad, worse than I thought."

After taking care of business, she started poking around the upstairs. At first she was merely looking for Clint, but then the charm of the old house called to her. Wainscoting on the walls, sloped ceilings, dormer windows. As a child, she'd lived in a house much like this one. Then her parents had been murdered, and her whole life had turned inside out.

When she opened a closet, she found a gold mine—clothes! She could get out of the ridiculous, damp things she was wearing. She selected a pair of jeans that looked like they might fit, plus a cotton polo-type shirt in a cranberry color. There was even a pair of old canvas flats.

That should do it, she thought as she stripped down to her panties. The jeans were snug, and she had to roll up the cuffs; the shoes were too large but wearable. If only she could find a hairbrush and her moisturizer, she might feel human again!

She wandered downstairs. "Clint?"

No answer. Surely if he'd gone somewhere, he would have told her. But he was nowhere to be found. A look out front confirmed her fears. The car was gone.

Panic washed over her. Had he abandoned her? Had she interfered with his plans by not escaping when he'd told her she was free to go? Oh, Lord, she hoped not. She needed him. And maybe he didn't realize it, but he needed her.

Despair was setting in when she heard what sounded like the whine of his 240Z. Relief flooded through her when she saw the burnt-orange car whipping down the driveway. A few hours earlier she'd have traded anything to see the last of him. Now she felt oddly anxious when he was out of her sight.

She actually ran out to the car to meet him. "Where did you go? You scared me to death, leaving me alone."

"Miss me?" he drawled. But when he saw that she

really had been worried, he straightened up. "I thought you'd be asleep for ages. I needed to get a charger for the phone. And as long as I was out, I picked up a few groceries, and—where'd you get the clothes?"

"I found 'em."

"Nice color. Looks good on you." His gaze roved over her in a thoroughly familiar way before he abruptly looked away.

Marissa felt herself blushing. She knew he could see her nipples through the shirt. She wasn't used to going braless. But, shoot, he'd seen her almost naked. Why his frank perusal now should bother her was a mystery.

She grabbed one of the grocery sacks. Her blood was thrumming through her veins in a strange way. It was probably just exhaustion, she told herself.

"Do you know where they took Rusty?" she asked as they went inside.

"Ah, no. But the closest hospital would probably be Clear Lake, or maybe Bayshore in Pasadena."

"Can we call and check up on him? I mean, you said your cell phone was untraceable, right?"

"Yeah. Each time a call is made, the signal goes through half a dozen relays. It'll show up as a different location each time on a caller ID, or even a professional trace. Still, we have to be careful."

"Please? I'll keep the call short. I'll just check on Rusty's condition." She needed to know if she'd done him serious harm. If so, she intended to give herself up to the police.

"Well, I guess it'd be okay." Clint set his bag of groceries on the kitchen counter. "The phone's in the car, charging up." He handed her the keys.

She looked at the keys, then at him. "You trust me with the keys to your car? Aren't you afraid I'll take off?"

He pretended to consider her words, then shook his head. "Nah. I'm getting ready to make cheese omelets."

Marissa suddenly realized she hadn't eaten anything since the night before, and then, she'd had only a few graham crackers. "For the cheese omelets, I'll stick around. Back in a minute."

She practically skipped down the porch stairs toward the haphazardly parked car. She would feel so much better if she knew Rusty was okay, even if he was a cold-blooded worm hardly worth the cellular charge. She called Information to get numbers for both hospitals Clint had mentioned, scribbling them on her hand with a ballpoint pen from the glove compartment.

Bayshore's emergency room didn't have any idea what she was talking about, so she tried Clear Lake Hospital.

"Yes, I'm trying to find information on a patient that might have been brought in—head injury, found in a motel room?"

"Let me check, one moment please."

Marissa counted the seconds. What if Rusty had told some wild story when he woke up? Were the police tracing the call even now? If the FBI was brought in, they might put two and two together and come up with this safe house—

"Ma'am?"

"Yes?" Marissa squeaked.

"An ambulance did come in a couple of hours ago

with a case like you described, but the patient got up and walked out."

Thank God.

"Ma'am? Could I get some information from you? We need some insurance information, and the police would like to talk to this man—"

Marissa hung up. The police. She'd never had a real fondness for law enforcement people. They ran around in that same shadowy world as the criminals she despised, and she'd never wanted anything to do with either group. But she'd never felt afraid of the police before. In this situation, however, she instinctively knew that to bring them in would be a disaster. Clint had committed innumerable felonies in the past twenty-four hours. He would end up in jail, and that would never do, not if her embryonic plan was going to work.

Jimmy was the key. The temptation to call him was strong. If she could let him know that she was safe . . . but no, that would be stupid. It was only another hour until Clint was supposed to call him. She would wait until then.

A delicious odor greeted her when she went back into the house. Her stomach rumbled. Cheese omelets. And toast, she definitely smelled toast.

"Any luck?" Clint asked over his shoulder as he tended the eggs.

"He's okay. Apparently he got up and left the emergency room without even telling his name."

"Great," Clint said without much enthusiasm. "I mean, he's my ex-brother-in-law, and I guess I should be glad he's not dead, but I'm not exactly comforted by the fact that he's running around, probably ready to kill both of us."

Marissa felt a shiver. "He doesn't know about this house, does he?"

"No. I told him my plans only as he needed to know them."

"What about Rachelle? Does she know about the house?"

Clint shook his head. "I never confided anything in her."

Marissa thought there was a certain sadness in that admission. A husband and wife should share things.

Marissa set out paper plates and napkins and plastic utensils on the counter for their feast. Clint had thought of everything, even cups for their orange juice. Good thing, too, since the cupboards were bare.

"So," Clint said as he slid the second omelet onto a plate. "Earlier you said you had an idea, a way we could help each other. I'd sure like to hear it. 'Cause lately, my ideas haven't panned out worth dog-doo."

They carried their plates out onto the porch, where some rusted patio chairs provided the only available seating. Marissa settled down with her plate in her lap, then took a bite. It was heavenly. No omelet had ever tasted better. The man was gorgeous, and he could cook too.

"Okay," she said, gathering her thoughts. "Now, I know this is a little rough, but hear me out. I figure, if Eddie Constantine has decided to get rid of you, and he went to all that trouble to set you up, you have a real problem."

"No kidding."

"You either have to nail Eddie and his buddies—put 'em all in jail—or move to Peoria and change your name."

"What do you think I've been trying to do for the past eight months? I've been full-time on this investigation. I'd have taken Jimmy and Eddie and a score of others out ages ago, except that the Bureau wants more. They always want more." There was a definite trace of bitterness in his voice.

"Like what?"

"Like the guy Jimmy's been dealing with from a South American drug cartel. He's the big boss, the real target."

Marissa decided to ignore, for now, Clint's implication of Jimmy. She had her own theories about her brother's role in all this. "So, what you need is evidence."

"Yeah. We need a name, for starters. Someone to tail, someone to bug. This guy's been a real slippery character. We know he's out there because of the amount of cash that's been flowing through the Foxhunt. But we can't get a handle on where and when certain key transactions are taking place."

"What would help you?"

"Well . . . getting into the Foxhunt would help. I've collected enough evidence that I could get a search warrant with no problem, but that would alert the bad guys. Even if we found what we wanted, they would know what we found, and anyone implicated would slither away like cockroaches when you turn on the light."

Marissa shivered. "So you want to have a look around without anyone knowing."

"It couldn't hurt."

"Perfect. Jimmy can help."

Clint merely arched his eyebrows at her.

"Here's what we do. I'll call Jimmy and tell him I've escaped. We'll arrange for him to come pick me up. Then, once he shows up, we introduce him to you. You tell him what you need, and he helps you get it."

"Ah." Understanding dawned. *Here* was Marissa's angle. "And when the arrests are made and the indictments start raining down, Jimmy gets off scot-free. Is that what you had in mind?"

"Sort of." She drained her orange juice. "This is my theory. I think Jimmy's a patsy. I'm not saying he's lily white. Obviously he's been associating with scum, and if what you say about the Foxhunt is true, then he owns a strip club."

"It's true."

"So, he's involved in some penny-ante stuff. He might be taking a few kickbacks to look the other way. But as for him being a key figure in some huge drug-smuggling, money-laundering scheme, it simply couldn't be."

"Why not?" Family members were always the last to suspect. He'd seen it time and time again. "Everywhere I turn, Jimmy Gabriole's name comes up. He owns the cars, the boats, the planes, the buildings—everything."

Marissa shook her head. "I'd bet my left arm that Eddie really has control of all that stuff. He got Jimmy to put his name on all of it with that story about trying to keep his assets out of his ex-wife's hands, and Jimmy fell for it."

"He couldn't be that dumb."

Marissa nodded. "Yeah, he could be. I love my brother dearly, but—how do I say this nicely?—he's never been known for his IQ. Besides, friendship is everything to Jimmy. For as long as I can remember, that's all that mattered—being part of the gang, buying everybody drinks even if he couldn't afford it, having everybody love him. He just wants people to love him."

She sniffed back a tear. Poor, misguided Jimmy. Always a little overweight, a little slower. Kids made fun of him as a teenager, until he'd show up at school with a hundred-dollar bill or a new, fast car—little presents from their father. Then he was everyone's best friend.

Clint was silent, digesting what she'd told him. Then he asked, "If Jimmy is so crazy about having friends, what makes you think he'd turn on them?"

Marissa knew this was the weakest part of her argument, but she pushed ahead. "If he knew what was really going on—especially that Eddie was planning to kill a cop—he would have no trouble changing his allegiance. He's a weak man, but please, you have to believe me, he doesn't have a truly mean or evil bone in his body. If you could convince him that he was really doing the FBI a service—you know, make him feel important—he would do everything in his power to help you, I'm sure of it."

"Even if it means going to jail?"

Marissa flinched. To her dismay, she could feel more tears building in her eyes. Jimmy wasn't a bad person. He didn't deserve to be locked up. Prison would break him, utterly. He wasn't strong enough for that.

She forced herself to ask what was on her mind. "If—

if he cooperated fully, couldn't you get him a suspended sentence or something?"

"That would be for the DA to decide, not me." Clint's tone was businesslike. But when he looked at her, she saw compassion. He understood, because he was going through the same thing. She'd forced him to acknowledge that his ex-wife, the woman he once purportedly loved and trusted, had turned on him like a cornered rat. Losing faith in someone you cared for—or having it snatched away from you—was one tough pill to swallow. And they were both swallowing with all their strength.

That moment of empathy, more than anything that had passed between them, convinced her that she had a lot to learn about Clint—hell, she didn't even know his last name.

Clint stood abruptly, crumpling his paper plate. "Your brother's in a lot of trouble. I don't want to soft-pedal it to you."

"I know."

"But . . . I could put in a good word for him. I guess."

She could tell what that offer cost him, and her heart swelled. She was on her feet, her tears breaking through the dam. "That would be great. That's all I'm asking." Before she could consider her actions, she'd closed the space between them and put her arms around him. "He's not a bad person," she said, still sobbing. "You'll see when you meet him. You'll see."

Reluctantly, it seemed, Clint returned the embrace.

He sifted her hair through his fingers and patted her back. "Don't cry, Marissa. I can't stand women crying."

"I'll t-try to stop." She pulled away slightly, embarrassed that her tears had made a damp spot on Clint's T-shirt. She was just so tired, that was all.

Clint looked down at her, then took her chin and tilted her face toward his. "Try a little harder, okay?" Then he touched his lips to hers.

SEVEN

Immediately, Marissa forgot all about crying. At the first tentative touch, a bolt of awareness crackled through her body. Their mouths locked, and something elemental passed between them. Marissa didn't fight it. She swayed against him, her knees rubbery, her breathing erratic.

Oh, no. How could her feelings for Clint be so strong, so fast? This was foolish. She was grateful, nothing more. But her thoughts blurred into one another as other sensations took over her brain—the taste of Clint, the feel of his powerful arms locked around her as if he never wanted to let her go.

She could have stood that way with him all day. She forgot about Jimmy, about her plan, about her safety, and certainly her sanity. It was Clint who stopped, who lifted his head, gulping in the humid coastal air. Then he looked at her again. Fire blazed in his eyes. They reminded her of lightning-limned thunderclouds. But there was something else in his gaze, something akin to fear.

Not that she imagined for a moment that Clint was afraid of her, but something about the kiss had spooked him.

"What the hell was that?" he wanted to know.

"If you don't know, then you've been missing something in your life," she quipped, though she felt far from humorous. She just didn't know how else to handle it. If she shrugged the whole thing off, he would think she went around kissing people that way all the time. And if she told him what she was really feeling—that the kiss had been the most soul-stirring, mind-boggling experience she'd ever participated in, he would think *she* was the naive one, totally lacking in worldliness.

Still holding her in a light embrace, he narrowed his eyes speculatively. "Maybe I have at that."

She pulled away abruptly, clearing her throat, looking everywhere but at him. "Why don't I go clean up the kitchen?"

"There's no time," Clint said, his voice rough. The sound of it skittered down each and every one of her nerve endings. "We need to decide where you should be when you call Jimmy. Then we have to decide exactly what you'll say to him. We have to get your story straight."

Marissa nodded, her spirits sagging a bit. The consummate professional, Clint could turn off his emotions easily. Back to business. Of course, she was the one who'd mentioned kitchen cleaning. She should be grateful that he was going along with her plan. "We should call him before noon. From somewhere besides here, I'm guessing. Maybe we should get a move on."

"Let's do it, then. You have my keys."

Sheepishly, Marissa fished in the tight jeans pocket for the car keys she'd never returned. When she handed them over, her fingers brushed against Clint's, and again there was that frisson of awareness, like static electricity.

Now she was the one getting spooked. This was a man who resorted to force when he wanted something. She should be repulsed, not attracted. But she *was* attracted, and had been from the very moment she laid eyes on him. The very thing that had frightened her—his power over her—had also drawn her.

The really scary part was, he still had power over her. He'd freed her. If she walked away and never looked back, he wouldn't stop her. Yet, she couldn't.

"What if Eddie is listening in when I call Jimmy?" Marissa asked as they hurtled down the highway toward Houston.

They'd been going over their strategy. Clint wasn't wild about Marissa's plan. He liked the part where he got his hands on Jimmy Gabriole, but the rest of it seemed kind of half-baked. She'd been right about one thing, though. Everything depended on Jimmy. Once Clint talked to him, he would have to make the decision as to if, and how much, they could trust him.

It also hadn't escaped his attention that he was going directly against Bureau orders by moving ahead with Marissa's proposition. McCormick would never condone this setup. He wouldn't believe Marissa's story to begin with. He would want to pull in Rusty. He would want to drag the bay for the sunken *Phen-Hu.* Most significantly, he would want to throw Clint's butt in jail, and rightly so.

Meanwhile, their window of opportunity for meeting with Jimmy and securing his cooperation would close.

"I'm almost certain Eddie *will* be there when you call," Clint answered. He'd been thinking this angle through. "If Eddie set me up, then he must be the 'friend' Jimmy referred to, the one who knows where Rachelle is. Yeah, I suspect he'll be listening in on the phone call."

Marissa nodded her agreement. "I was afraid you would say that. But you're right. If Jimmy turned to Eddie for help, Eddie no doubt put on a big act, pretending to be the supportive friend, offering advice, manipulating things his way. And if Rusty's talked to them—"

"I don't think he has."

"Why not?"

"If he was trying to make points with the big guys, he didn't succeed. In fact, he screwed up pretty badly. He doesn't want them to know how badly. In fact, he'd probably rather they didn't know of his involvement at all."

"Oh, but I think they already knew. He said he'd talked to Rachelle right before he rented the *Phen-Hu.* So he probably told her what was going on, don't you think?"

Another knife pierced Clint's heart. Rachelle again. He still found it nearly impossible to believe Rachelle had signed his death warrant. But he couldn't ignore the evidence Marissa had presented to him. It all dovetailed together so nicely.

"I'm sorry," Marissa said. "I don't mean to keep throwing her in your face. It must hurt—"

"She's not that important to me," Clint said, a bold-faced lie he knew wouldn't fool Marissa. Still, it stopped the amateur psychoanalysis she'd been about to give him. Hell, yeah, it hurt. He wasn't in love with Rachelle, but he'd believed they held a certain loyalty to each other.

He'd deal with the pain later. Emotions had no place in the middle of a critical operation.

"Anyway," Marissa continued, "we need to convince Jimmy to come alone when he picks me up."

"It shouldn't be a problem," Clint said. "All you have to do is tell him to pick you up at FBI headquarters, that you've been there all morning spilling your guts about this nutcase agent who kidnapped you. I guarantee Eddie won't be within ten miles of that place. In fact, I'll be surprised if Jimmy agrees to come there."

Marissa's eyes flashed dangerously, as they did any time she was forced to defend her brother. "You just watch. He'll be there in a New York minute without even blinking."

Clint hoped she was right.

Downtown Houston was pretty desolate on Sundays. Clint passed up the Bureau garage and parked on the street. There was a pay phone on the corner.

"You ready?" he asked Marissa.

Marissa wiped her palms on the legs of her jeans. "Ready."

Clint put Rusty's gun, newly reloaded, in the waist-band of his jeans and pulled his shirt hem out to hide the weapon as they got out of the car.

"Do you absolutely have to carry that thing?" Marissa asked.

"Yes." Didn't she realize he was doing it for her protection? So much for his "no guns" promise to himself. All bets were off from the time he'd kissed Marissa. He might have acted slightly protective toward her before, but now he felt like he would tackle a rhinoceros barehanded to keep her safe. Besides, when had she developed qualms about carrying a weapon? The gun stayed.

"Figures," she muttered.

Her obvious disgust really bothered him. She'd painted him with the same brush she used for Eddie and his ilk. Clint wanted to argue that he wasn't like them—he was one of the good guys. But given his recent history, he figured he'd be wasting his breath with that argument. He grabbed the cell phone, stuffed it in his back pocket, and slammed the door.

He walked close to her as they made their way down the sidewalk. He had no reason to believe anyone was watching them, but Clint was superalert nonetheless.

When they reached the phone, Marissa took a deep breath and deposited a quarter.

Jimmy answered his home number on the first ring with a cautious "hello?"

Marissa's heart thudded almost painfully. "Jimmy?"

"God, Marissa? Are you all right?"

"Yeah." She did her best to sound like a traumatized woman. "Jimmy, I escaped. I need you to come get me."

"Oh, thank God! Sure, sissy, sure. You just tell me where."

"I'm downtown, in the twenty-five hundred block of Jester. Listen, Jimmy, the guy that hijacked your boat—"

"It's okay, baby, we know all about him."

Jimmy's use of "we" didn't reassure her. "Oh, good. He's really crazy. You didn't pay him any ransom money or anything, did you?"

"No. He didn't want money. This whole thing was about him being crazy for some chick. Eddie was gonna help me out with this thing—God, Marissa, I was scared to death. You sure you're okay?"

"Yes. He didn't hurt me, and he's not following me or anything. I called nine-one-one, and the police picked me up and took me to the FBI headquarters downtown. 'Cause this guy was an FBI agent, you know?"

"Yeah, that's what Eddie said. I hope they're gonna arrest the lowlife. You, uh, told the FBI the whole story?"

"Everything."

"Good. Maybe I'll get my boat back. Look, Sophia and I'll come get you, okay? I don't like leaving you on no downtown street corner on a Sunday."

"Okay. But only you two, okay? Leave Eddie out of this. I look a mess, and I don't want anyone else to see me."

"Sure thing, sissy. Give us twenty or thirty minutes." He hung up.

So did Marissa. She turned toward Clint, finding herself almost lip to lip with him again. She quickly took a half-step backward. "So, what'd you think?"

"He's coming, like you said. And from the way he was

talking, it sounded as if Eddie Constantine was the one who knew what was going on."

Marissa nodded, giving him an I-told-you-so look.

"Okay, here's the plan. I'll wait in my car. When you get in Jimmy's car, you signal me if Jimmy and Sophia are alone."

"How do I do that?"

"Put your left hand up and smooth your hair before you get in. Yes, like that," he said as she tried out the gesture. "Then I'll tail Jimmy's car to make sure no one is following him. After about ten minutes, you ask Jimmy to pull over at a gas station or someplace. Claim you have to use the restroom."

Marissa nodded. She felt like a traitor, using all this subterfuge to get her own brother alone. But Clint was giving Jimmy the benefit of the doubt. The least she could do was follow these simple directions. He seemed to know what he was doing.

"At the gas station, or wherever you stop, you watch for my car," he continued. "I'll give you a thumbs-up if everything's okay. If anyone besides me is following, I'll give you a thumbs-down. That means you're to get directly into my car, no questions asked, and the deal's off. Okay?"

Marissa bristled. "My brother isn't going to hurt me!"

"No, but his friends might." Clint brushed a strand of hair off her forehead, a tender expression overcoming him. Then he seemed to remember himself, and pulled back. "They have a lot to lose in this operation—millions and millions of dollars, and someone's going to be doing jail time too. They're not nice people. If they have even a slight suspicion that you know something useful, they won't let you simply walk away. My guess is that Eddie already ordered Jimmy to bring you to him for a little conversation, at the very least."

Marissa shivered, despite the fact that the sun was warming things up pretty quickly. What Clint said made sense. He'd been on this case for—what had he said—eight months? Marissa knew almost nothing about it. She had to bow to his expertise.

She nodded. "Okay. I smooth my hair with my left hand if Jimmy and Sophia are alone in the car. What if there *is* someone else there?"

"Don't get in the car. Seriously," he added when she opened her mouth to object.

She gave a frustrated hmph. "All right. I ask to go to the bathroom after ten minutes. Thumbs-up, I return to the car with you and make introductions. Thumbs-down, I get into your car. But what if he sees you following? There's not a lot of traffic, and that car of yours isn't exactly anonymous."

"It could happen, I suppose." Clint frowned. "Okay. If Jimmy realizes he's being followed, open a window and wave or something. I'll drop back. Stop at a gas station the way we planned before, and use a pay phone to call me on the cellular. Then wait for me. I already gave you the number, right?"

"Oh, Clint, this is all so cloak-and-dagger!" He was scaring her. She didn't enjoy behaving like some two-bit Mata Hari in a B movie.

"This is standard undercover stuff," he assured her. "I'll be with you. I won't let anything happen to you."

His voice was low, velvety, almost seductive. And, dammit, why did she find it so reassuring?

"That's a pretty glib promise," she quipped, "coming from a man who almost drowned me last night."

"I wouldn't blame you if you didn't believe me," he said, completely serious. He looked down at her with those unusual eyes, which right now looked like a soft summer rain cloud. He touched her face. "I can't believe you've stuck around this long. If I were you, I might be rooting for Eddie to win."

Rather than step away, as she knew she should do, she closed her eyes and savored his touch. "Don't say that, not even in jest," she said. "I despise Eddie Constantine, always have. He's been the worst possible influence on Jimmy. Prison is too good for him, but I still can't wait to see him there."

"Amen to that." Clint brushed his lips against her forehead, so quickly and lightly that she almost believed she'd imagined it, and trotted back to where the Z was parked. The windows were tinted, so no one would notice him. Even though she knew he was watching over her, she felt suddenly alone, vulnerable.

Marissa found a wall to perch against while she waited for Jimmy, the longest fifteen minutes of her life. She counted the cars that went by—not too many. What were the chances that Clint could avoid detection?

She was relieved when Jimmy's BMW pulled up to the curb, but apprehensive too. She hoped she remembered her role. She hoped she didn't say anything that would give her position away before she was ready. Jimmy was sure to question her about the events of the last fourteen hours. She tried to see inside, but his windows were also tinted.

To her surprise, Jimmy jumped out from the driver's seat and threw his arms around her. "Oh, baby, little sister, are you a sight for sore eyes." Then he held her away from him and inspected her from head to toe. "You sure that jerk didn't hurt you? I mean it, now. If he did anything to you—"

"No, Jimmy. He didn't hurt me." Clint had said to stick with the truth as much as possible, so she wouldn't have to remember what lies she told. "Please, can we go? I haven't had any sleep."

"Sure, sissy, sure." He opened the back door for her. Marissa quickly peered inside. The backseat was empty. Sophia sat in the passenger seat. Marissa paused, smoothed her hair back with her left hand, and climbed in.

"Marissa!" Sophia squealed, reaching one of her soft, perfectly manicured hands back between the bucket seats to touch her sister-in-law. "We've been so worried, sweetie. I knew you shouldn'ta turned down that lobsta dinner."

Lord, it seemed an eternity ago that she was looking forward to that quiet couple of hours to read and nurse her nausea. "Thanks, Sophia. I'm fine, really, just a little tired." She noted the time on the digital clock in the dash, so she would know when ten minutes had passed.

"So, how did you escape from that maniac?" Sophia wanted to know. "We're dyin', here! You're so brave and clever."

By now, Jimmy had slid behind the wheel and locked

the doors. He hit the accelerator. "Don't pester the girl, Sophia. You heard her. She's pooped."

"Oh, I don't mind telling you," she said, though Clint had cautioned her to say as little as possible to avoid tripping on her own lies. "He stole your boat, and then he met up with an accomplice and put me on another boat—"

"An accomplice?" Jimmy interrupted. "Who?"

"Well, I don't know," Marissa said, disturbed by the urgent tone in Jimmy's voice. Did he have more of a stake in this thing than he was letting on? "Just some guy. I didn't ever hear his name. Anyway, this other boat was a horrible, fishy-smelling thing. Then the storm got worse, and there was a fire—"

"A fire!" Sophia squealed.

"And the boat sank and we had to swim for shore," Marissa concluded, all in one breath. "They dragged me to this cheap motel, and then the first guy—"

"Nichols," Jimmy supplied. "Clint Nichols, the bastard. According to Eddie, he's some piece of work."

So, that was his last name, Marissa thought. "Well, whoever he was, he left me alone with the second guy. The second guy fell asleep, and I hit him over the head with a lamp and got out of there."

"Oh, Marissa, that was so brave!" Sophia gushed. "I never would have had the guts to—"

"Pipe down, Sophia," Jimmy said brusquely.

Marissa's stomach turned; she'd never heard Jimmy say a cross word to his bride. Again, she wondered if Clint had been right about Jimmy, that he had more riding on the outcome of the FBI's investigation than she knew about.

"Marissa," Jimmy said, "Eddie's a little bit worried about what you told the FBI. You know, he has to be careful about these things. He's not exactly a choirboy."

"I know," Marissa said, not even bothering to hide her disgust. She'd never made her animosity toward Eddie a secret. "But what's *he* got to worry about?"

"You mean, his name didn't come up?"

Marissa pretended confusion. "No. Why would it? I mean, this Clint guy was trying to get money out of you, right?"

"Is that what he told you?"

"He wasn't exactly chummy with me, but he mentioned once or twice that he wanted to 'do business' with you."

"And he didn't mention this woman to you? This girl named Rachelle?"

Marissa gave her brother a blank stare in the rearview mirror. "No. Who's she?"

Jimmy shook his head, looking decidedly relieved. "Ah, never mind. This Nichols is a nutcase, like you said. He's been poking around in Eddie's business—probably some trumped-up thing his ex-wife started—and he went off the deep end."

"But how did *you* get involved?" Marissa knew Clint would be very upset over her conducting her own interrogation, but the question had been burning inside her. She had to know.

Jimmy shrugged. "Damned if I know. Probably has something to do with my owning the Foxhunt. Let's just be glad it's over and done with. The FBI's gonna arrest this clown, huh?"

"They said they would."

"Good. The sooner the better. Meanwhile, Sophia and I want you to come stay with us. You'll be safer."

"Yeah, okay. Thanks, you two. I don't know what I'd do without you." She checked the clock. Nine minutes, and Jimmy hadn't said a thing about any strange orange cars following. She decided to make her move; otherwise, they'd be getting on the freeway. "Um, Jimmy, I have to use the restroom. There's a gas station up ahead. Pull in, will you?"

"Oh, goody, I hafta go too," Sophia said. "Jimmy don't ever stop for me."

Great. This wasn't a contingency plan Marissa and Clint had discussed.

Jimmy pulled into the station, which was attached to a convenience store. The restrooms apparently were inside. She didn't see the orange Z as she got out, so she had no choice but to go inside with Sophia on her heels and use the facilities.

What if something had happened to Clint? she wondered furiously. On the way, she hadn't dared look out the rear window for fear of alerting Jimmy to their escort. She'd assumed that Clint was back there.

Relief swamped her as she and Sophia exited the convenience store. Clint was parked right outside, the driver's window opened. He grinned and gave her a big thumbs-up.

This was too easy, she thought. Maybe she ought to

reconsider her vocation. She would make a damn good undercover cop.

She smiled back at him.

"Ooh, goodness, who's he?" Sophia cooed, automatically smoothing her bleached blond hair.

"An old friend," Marissa murmured.

Clint walked right up to them. "Afternoon, ladies. Marissa, how've you been? Haven't seen you in a while."

"Fine, Cl—" Damn! She'd almost blown it. "Clarence. So good to see you. This is my sister-in-law, Sophia. And I want you to come meet my brother."

"Love to."

Marissa opened the back door of the BMW, letting Clint climb in ahead of her.

"Hey, what the—" Jimmy started to object.

"It's okay, Jimmy," Marissa quickly said. "He's an old friend of mine. He wanted to meet you."

As soon as all doors were closed and locked, Clint held out his hand. "Jimmy Gabriole. Man, have I heard a lot about you."

Jimmy smiled uncertainly, accepting Clint's handshake. "And you are . . ."

"Clint Nichols," he replied with a friendly smile. "I have a gun in my other hand, trained right at your back, so don't make any sudden moves."

EIGHT

Sophia screamed. "Oh, my God, it's that nutcase FBI agent! We're all gonna die!"

"Quiet!" Clint barked. He glanced over at Marissa for help, but she wouldn't meet his gaze as the bitter taste of betrayal rose in her throat. How could he do this? He hadn't said anything about pulling the gun.

Was it all a scam, then? Was everything he'd told her a pack of lies? Jeez, not only had she blown any chance she had of escape, but she'd drawn Jimmy and Sophia into mortal danger too.

Clint slowly released Jimmy's hand. "Put both hands on the steering wheel, please, and keep them there. Jimmy, are there any weapons in the car?"

"For cripe's sake," Jimmy said. "Marissa, what's going on?"

She looked over at Clint. "Well, um . . ."

"Would you mind telling him?" Clint asked impatiently. "Things are a little tense here, in case you hadn't noticed."

"They wouldn't have been tense if you didn't have that stupid gun!" she said, wishing she had the guts to take it away from him the way he'd taken hers away.

"I'm trying to keep myself from being shot," he said through gritted teeth. "I'm willing to bet there's at least one other gun in this car."

Probably two, Marissa conceded silently. Jimmy always had a gun in the car, and Sophia probably had one in her purse. They both were qualified to carry a concealed weapon, as Marissa was. "Okay," she said, reaching a decision. She would have to be the one to defuse this situation. "Everybody just calm down. Sophia, stop crying. No one is going to die." She reached between the seat and opened the console. There was Jimmy's pearl-handled pistol, an old Colt similar to hers but larger. It had belonged to their father. She grabbed it and handed it to Clint.

"Marissa, what are you doing?" Jimmy demanded.

"Clint's only here to talk," she said. "The faster and better you cooperate, the sooner he'll be done with his questions and be gone. Sophia, hand me your purse."

"But—"

"Just do it, baby," Jimmy said, sounding resigned.

Still sobbing, Sophia handed Marissa her large, black designer bag. Marissa fished inside, found a blue steel nine millimeter, and handed it to Clint. He was already armed with enough bullets to kill them all. What were a few more?

Clint methodically emptied the guns of ammunition,

then set them on the floor. "Thank you, Marissa." His own gun had vanished.

"Somebody around here has to show some sense," she grumbled.

"I'm sorry," he said. "I had to do it this way. I'd be insane to sit in a car with two loaded guns and announce to your brother that I'm the one who kidnapped you, stole his boat, threatened to attack you."

"All right, I see your point," she retorted crossly. "Let's just get on with this, okay?"

"Fine. Jimmy, take I-45 south to Telephone Road. We'll go someplace comfortable to talk. The gun's put away."

"I'll drive wherever you want," Jimmy said. "But start talking now. Whatever beef you got with me, I wanta solve it." He pulled his car out of the parking lot with a squeal of tires.

"Okay. Let's start with the fact that I've collected enough dirt on you to put you away for a lot of years."

"Like what?" Jimmy tried to sound cocky, but he came off sounding frightened instead.

"Tax evasion, for starters."

Marissa's head was spinning again. Clint hadn't told her any of this. She'd thought they would have a nice, friendly little chat. If she'd had even an inkling that Clint would come on like a Gestapo agent, she never would have hatched this plan.

Jimmy actually laughed at the accusation. "That's bull. Marissa does my taxes. Ask her."

"The tax stuff is only the beginning," Clint continued relentlessly. "Your name is listed on the title for a certain private jet, several automobiles, and a warehouse, all of which are known to be involved in cocaine transactions of various magnitudes. Then there's the Foxhunt."

"Hey, my club is a perfectly legitimate business!" Jimmy objected. "We obey every code to the letter."

"I'm aware of that. I'm also aware that the cash deposits made from that business far exceed the norm. And that every dollar bill is reeking with cocaine. You could get a buzz just from holding those bills up to your nose."

Jimmy went silent.

"Look, Gabriole, if you aren't the brains behind a very large drug and money-laundering operation, then someone has gone to a lot of trouble to make it appear that you are."

Still, Jimmy said nothing.

"It's not Jimmy," Sophia said with quiet certainty. "He would *never* do what you're talking about. He ain't like that. He's a decent, kind man who wouldn't hurt—"

"Then who?" Clint asked, cutting her off.

Hell, Marissa thought, this was like shooting fish in a barrel. With her penchant for chatter, Sophia would blab everything. She would either exonerate Jimmy . . . or hammer that final nail into his coffin. Marissa was ashamed that she wasn't entirely sure which was going to happen.

"It's Eddie, of course," Sophia said, looking to her husband for confirmation. "That lousy creep, Eddie Constantine. I never liked him, Jimmy. He always cops a feel when you're not looking."

"What? He does what?" Jimmy suddenly came alive with indignation. Cocaine, money laundering, it's all in a day's work, Marissa supposed. But someone feeling up his wife, that made Jimmy mad.

"He pinches me on the butt." She turned back to Clint. "Eddie's the one. He owns all that stuff, but he gets Jimmy to put his name on everything. He *said* it was so his ex-wife wouldn't try to grab stuff from him, but now I see what his real intentions are. He wants Jimmy to take the fall for him."

"C'mon, Sophia," Jimmy said. "Eddie's my best friend. I've known him since high school."

"He's a jerk," Sophia insisted, "and it's high time you quit covering for him. He uses you. Everybody sees that but you."

The knot of tension in Marissa's stomach eased. At least her brother and sister-in-law were saying and doing everything she'd told Clint they would. Her theory about Eddie Constantine was dead-on—there was no way Clint could doubt her now.

Not that she gave the man any credit for common sense, but surely he could see that her plan was sound. He and Jimmy could save each other only by working together to defeat Eddie—if they could keep from killing each other for however long it took.

Clint had blown it with Marissa. Maybe pulling the gun had been overkill. But he'd once had a buddy killed in a drug deal gone bad when he climbed into the backseat of a car. Better safe than sorry.

Still, Clint hadn't realized how shocked she would be. Judging from the invisible poisoned darts she was shooting in his direction straight from her blazing eyes, he could never undo the damage. She would never again allow him to kiss her.

Not that it mattered, he told himself, even as the memory of what her lips did to him sent an electric charge coursing through his body. He had no business getting the least bit involved with her. When this all came out in the wash, he was probably going to jail. The fact that he'd had physical contact—no matter how brief— with his hostage would not go down well.

At least there was some good news. His interrogation of Gabriole was going like clockwork. Okay, so it was a little unconventional, and nothing he'd learned so far would stand up in court. Right now he needed information, not evidence. When he knew what he needed to know, he would go back to the Bureau and let someone there direct the next step.

Not that he wouldn't love to be in on the kill. But it was kind of hard to run an operation from a prison cell.

He asked more questions. Jimmy and Sophia gave him answers, and a lot of what they said made sense. The tension lessened. Clint revised, and re-revised, his thinking.

"You got any food in this safe house we're going to?" Jimmy asked. The conversation had wound down. Clint was giving him time to digest the severity of the situation.

"Yeah," Sophia put in. "My stomach is rumbling like there's an earth mover in there."

Clint had to admit, he liked Jimmy's *wife du jour*. After she got over her hysteria, she'd proved gutsy, not to mention informative. Turned out she'd known Eddie almost as long as Jimmy had, and she was chattier by far than her reticent husband, who was still having trouble with the concept of ratting on his best friend.

"I bought some groceries this morning," he said. "The furniture is a little on the skimpy side—"

"Hah, what furniture?" Marissa interjected. It was the first thing she'd said in a long time. "The house is completely empty."

"All right, so it's not a luxury hotel," Clint said. "It's big and it's quiet. We don't have to worry about anyone disturbing us there or listening in."

"Listening in to what?" Jimmy wanted to know.

"To our plans, Jimmy. You and I, we're going to figure out how to bring your friend Eddie down."

"Wait a minute," Jimmy objected. "I'll answer your questions 'cause you have a gun and I don't, but there's no way I'm conspiring with you to arrest my best friend."

"For God's sake, Jimmy," Marissa exploded. "The man is a cold-blooded killer. He was planning to kill Clint. He still wants to. And if you don't stop him, you might as well be pulling the trigger yourself."

"Might be doing the world a favor," Jimmy muttered. "Clint Nichols isn't exactly my favorite person, and if it's the last thing I do, I'll repay him for what he did to you, sis, not to mention my boat."

Clint recognized empty bravado when he heard it. Jimmy might be talking tough, but he drove to the safe house as instructed.

As they all climbed out of the car, Clint took all three guns and deposited them in Jimmy's trunk. "I want a level playing field," he said as Jimmy watched, surprised. "I don't have any other weapons, not on me or in the house. Marissa can vouch for that."

"What about the knife?" Marissa asked.

He'd forgotten about that. It was still strapped to his ankle. It took some doing to finally wiggle the holster out from the hem of his jeans leg. He tossed the blade and sheath into the trunk, then slammed the lid. He then handed the keys to Jimmy. He hoped they were at a point that he didn't have to worry about Gabriole doing anything stupid.

Marissa and Sophia walked ahead of the two men, into the house. By silent, mutual agreement, Jimmy and Clint stopped on the porch and dropped into the two chairs. Jimmy fumbled for the cigarettes in his shirt pocket. With hands slightly trembling, he lit one, took a drag, then slowly exhaled.

"What do you really want from me, Nichols? I know you find it hard to believe, but everything I've been telling you is true. I'm not involved in all this stuff you're talking about—drugs, money laundering, killing. I don't know what I could possibly do to help you."

Clint decided to bring out the big guns. "Well, you'd better think of something fast, 'cause at this point, you're every bit as expendable to Eddie as I am." And he told Jimmy about Rachelle.

"Don't you see?" he concluded. "Eddie was hoping I'd go after you, and *you'd* be the one to kill me. It would keep the blood off his hands. And if you got killed or arrested, even better. You were his sacrificial lamb."

Jimmy stared out into the front yard, lost in thought

for a long time, the cigarette burning away. Finally he said, "What happens if I want out of this right now?"

"I arrest you on the spot. I couldn't risk your going back to Eddie and telling him the things I've told you. An eight-month investigation would go down the tubes. Once you're in jail, I'll personally see to it that you're fully prosecuted for every possible offense."

Jimmy tugged at his collar. "And the alternative?"

"Help me get the evidence I need to arrest not just Eddie, but the man he deals with. When I have that, I can move in and shut this pipeline down."

"And me?"

"I'll be honest. I can't make any promises. But if everything you say is true, your involvement in these crimes is minimal. Your cooperation with me won't go unnoticed. I can put in a good word, and there's a chance you won't do any time."

"Jeez, not much of a choice."

Clint couldn't help but feel sorry for the man. He was guilty of gullibility more than anything, and now he had to face the fact that a lifelong friend had betrayed him. Clint knew what Jimmy was going through. Exactly.

Jimmy looked up with an expression of decisiveness and tossed his cigarette butt over the porch railing. "All right, you got it, whatever you want. I'm at your service. But first, I think you should know, Eddie's expecting a call from me. He wants a full report on what Marissa told the cops."

"Is he tracing his calls?"

"He has caller ID at his house, but I can probably get him on his cell phone."

Clint pulled the little portable phone out of his back pocket. "Do it. Tell him Marissa didn't know anything, not even my name. All she knew was that some crazy FBI agent kidnapped her and was trying to get something from you, but she didn't know what. Got that?"

Jimmy nodded. "What if he asks where I am?"

"Tell him it's none of his business. You don't want to be disturbed until tomorrow." It was the only answer Clint could think of. If Jimmy mentioned a particular place, Eddie might get it in his head to check on Marissa in person.

"Okay." With a visible shudder, Jimmy started dialing.

"So what's really going on with you and this FBI guy?" Sophia wanted to know. She and Marissa were in the kitchen, making sandwiches. "How come you're on his side?"

"I'm not on his side, exactly," Marissa answered. She was still fuming about that stupid gun. "I'm trying to keep Jimmy out of jail. Your loving husband has gotten in way over his head, and he doesn't even know it."

"It's that rotten Eddie," Sophia said, furiously spreading mayonnaise on a pumpernickel roll. "Men can be so stupid and disgusting."

"At least we're in agreement on that," Marissa said. "Hey, Sophia, were you ever, I mean, did you ever do, you know, exotic dancing?"

Sophia giggled. "You mean, was I a stripper? Yeah. Jimmy wanted me to quit before we got hitched, and I did. He said he didn't want no men but him lookin' at me." She giggled again.

Marissa tried not to be shocked. She'd always adored Sophia. Just because the girl had a somewhat unsavory past was no reason to stop loving her.

"But God gave me this body, and there's nothing wrong with letting other people appreciate it," Sophia elaborated.

"I'm sorry, Sophia," Marissa quickly said. "I don't mean to pass judgment. It's just that Jimmy always told me you were a waitress. Shoot, until this morning, I didn't even know the Foxhunt was a . . . gentlemen's club."

"It's a nice place to work. But I like being a lady of leisure better." Sophia popped an olive into her mouth.

"Did you know Rachelle?" Marissa asked.

Sophia rolled her eyes. "Yeah, sure, everybody knew her. Eddie's slut, last I heard. How do you know her?"

"I don't. But she's the one who implicated Jimmy in the first place. She's a paid informant, and apparently she's been passing on false tidbits to Clint about Jimmy."

Sophia had a few choice words to say about that. "Eddie again. He put her up to it. She's a cokehead, you know. She'll do anything for drugs. She turns tricks for guys I wouldn't even let stuff a dollar in my G-string."

Marissa's stomach turned. Her nice, neat world of numbers and tax returns had flipped off its axis, and now she was calmly discussing strippers and coke dealers and hookers as if they were everyday things for her. She'd taken such great pains to avoid all the unsavory things that her father had been involved in. Now there she was,

splat in the middle of the seamiest, darkest, most dangerous scenario she could envision.

It boggled her mind that people chose this way of life.
Undoubtedly her brother had tried his best to shield her
from it, but he was living with it every day. And
Clint . . . he claimed to be walking the right side of the
fence, but he was still part of that world.

How could she be so drawn to a man who deliberately
enmeshed himself in such things? Hell, she was more
than simply drawn to him. She was falling for him faster
than a loose pebble down a mine shaft. The thought of
Eddie actually succeeding with his plan to get rid of Clint
filled her with a fear so elemental, it actually made her
tremble.

And that was what kept her from simply walking
away.

Marissa and Sophia took plates of sandwiches outside
to the porch, where they found the two men with their
heads together, deep in conversation. The appearance of
food put a temporary halt to the conference. Marissa had
intended to simply leave the food and disappear again,
but Clint insisted the women stay.

Marissa found a sunny spot on the porch steps to sit
and munch her sandwich. She tried not to look at Clint,
because every time she saw him with that strong, un-
shaven jaw and those steely eyes, her stomach swooped,
and she knew her brother wasn't the only one in way, way
over his head.

"You ladies will be happy to know that Jimmy and I
have reached an agreement," Clint announced. "We'll be
working together until the arrests are made."

"Ooh, I like this already," Sophia said. "I've always wanted to be part of a conspiracy. What do I get to do?"

Jimmy rolled his eyes. "We're not *all* working together. It's dangerous, baby. That's why you're going to the airport this afternoon. You're going to visit your mother in Yonkers, and you'll stay there till this mess is over with."

Sophia opened her mouth to object, but she clamped it shut again when Jimmy shook his finger at her in warning. Instead she folded her arms and pouted.

"What about me?" Marissa asked, afraid of the answer.

"Is there someone you can stay with?" Clint asked. "I'd take you home, but I don't know how safe you'll be. I'm not sure who, at this point, is on Eddie's endangered list."

So, that was the plan. She'd gotten Clint together with Jimmy, and now she'd outlived her usefulness. It occurred to her that if she complacently let Clint cut her out of the picture, she would probably never see him again.

"There's no one I can stay with," she declared. "Besides, I figure you two macho men could use some help, whatever you're planning."

Clint was already shaking his head. "No way. You're staying firmly out of the line of fire."

She was on her feet, hands on hips. "You listen to me, Clint Nichols. I didn't ask to be included in this house party. I was minding my own business when you broke into my brother's boat, tied me up, and held me hostage. But I'm a part of it now. You may think you're calling all the shots, but I have news for you. This is a cooperative effort—and all my idea, I might add. I have a stake in this thing, too, and I intend to see it through."

Clint tried to placate her. "We're just going to do a little snooping at the Foxhunt tonight after hours," he said. "No big deal. I don't need an extra person to worry about."

"As if you've done such a sterling job of taking care of me so far?" Now she was really steamed. "Either I go with you, or I go straight to the FBI."

Clint's eyes narrowed. "I could tie you up here and leave you."

The air crackled with tension. Jimmy and Sophia watched wide-eyed, but neither of them intervened.

"Still solving your problems with brute force, I see."

He tried another tack. "Marissa, be reasonable. This is dangerous—"

"You've already put me in danger. Need I remind you, you almost drowned me? Or I could have burned to death tied to that bunk on the *Phen-Hu*."

That silenced Clint. He looked down at his plate.

"I've saved your bacon twice, Ace. You might just need me again." She'd played all her cards now. The idea of Clint actually *needing* her was laughable—and intriguing as hell.

"I'll think about it."

Marissa sat back down with a "hmmph."

Clint made several more calls on the cell phone, most of them while he paced up and down the driveway, out of earshot of the others. He made airline reservations for

Sophia, then called her a taxi despite Jimmy's objections that he could put his own wife on a plane.

"It's not inconceivable that someone could be looking for your car at the airport," Clint said quietly. "Eddie didn't sound too happy when you evaded his questions. He might get it into his head that you're planning to skip town."

"Yeah, okay," Jimmy finally said.

Sophia was teary-eyed when the taxi arrived. She gave Jimmy at least a dozen warnings to be careful, then kissed him passionately in full view of everyone before sprinting to the cab and climbing inside.

Marissa was tired, but the affectionate display moved her anyway. She'd always thought they made a cute couple. She hoped their marriage would survive whatever fate awaited them.

"I'm beat," Jimmy announced as the taxi pulled out of sight. "I was up all night, worrying about what you were doing to my sister." He curled his lip at Clint, but the snarl turned into a yawn. "Are there any beds in this joint?"

"Some pillows and blankets on the floor in one of the upstairs bedrooms," Marissa answered.

"Great. Sounds like a slumber party." He scuffed his way inside and slammed the screen door.

"That's where *I* was planning to crash," Clint said. "It's going to be another long night. We all need to get some sleep."

"Shouldn't someone stay awake? You know, to keep watch?"

Clint shrugged. "No one knows we're here. No one

besides Eddie is even interested in where we are right now, and for sure *he* doesn't know about this house."

"You're sure no one followed us?"

"Positive."

"And the FBI isn't going to come crashing in here to arrest everyone?"

"No."

He sounded pretty sure of himself. Then again, he'd been sure that Jimmy had kidnapped or killed Rachelle. "If we're both going to sleep, I want it to be in the same room."

His eyebrows shot up.

"That wasn't a proposition. I simply want to be behind you if bullets start to fly." That was something of a lie. Truthfully, with everything going on right now, she was just plain scared to be alone. She was utterly sure that Clint would protect her, even in sleep.

"All right." He didn't sound entirely pleased. "I think there might be another couple of pillows in that linen cupboard. We can crash down here in the living room."

Clint climbed the stairs, his shoulders slightly bent, his head bowed. She wasn't the only one suffering from exhaustion, she realized. He returned a moment later with one pillow, a long, king-sized one, then held it out to her with a shrug.

"You can have it," they both said at the same time.

"Why don't we share," Marissa said. "It's a big pillow. We'll each take one end."

He shrugged again. "Sure."

In moments they'd both flopped onto the floor, their bodies pointing away from each other. Marissa wiggled against the carpeted floor, trying to get comfortable. She punched the pillow a couple of times until she got it shaped right.

She'd thought herself a bit daring in suggesting they share a pillow, but this was pretty safe, she concluded. They couldn't touch even if they wanted to. They couldn't even see each other.

"Comfortable?" she asked.

He answered her with a soft snore.

She fell asleep almost instantly, and she slept like the proverbial log, despite the less-than-luxurious accommodations. When she woke some time later, she at least felt rested if a bit stiff. She yawned, stretched, then froze.

Someone was playing with her hair.

NINE

"I sure hope that's you, Clint."

Clint gave a low, deliberately sexy laugh. He'd slept hard and well and had awakened feeling halfway human. Unfortunately, human for him also meant male. He'd been achingly aware of Marissa lying a few feet away. He could hear her gentle breathing. He could smell her.

He'd turned over and found her dark, silky hair spilled in luxuriant disarray all over the pillow. Without giving it too much thought, he'd started combing it with his fingers. It really did feel like silk. He'd pressed his face against it, inhaling the fresh scent of motel soap and Marissa.

And then she'd caught him. Darn.

She flipped over onto her stomach, whipping her hair out of his light grasp, then propped her chin on her hand. "What are you doing?"

"Playing with your hair." Their faces were only inches apart.

"Why?"

"Because I woke up with it in my face," he fibbed. "You have really nice hair."

"Oh, please. My stylist would go into cardiac arrest if she could see me now."

"I like it. You know, before last night I'd never seen you. I'd seen pictures, and once I watched you through a telescope when you went to your brother's house. But I was still surprised when I saw you up close. I didn't realize how beautiful you were."

She narrowed her eyes suspiciously. "What *are* you doing? Why the come-on all of a sudden?"

Man, his technique must have slipped all to hell. He couldn't remember ever paying a woman such a compliment—an honest one at that—and having her throw it back in his face. "Guess it's been a long time since I was with a woman."

Judging from her frown, she didn't like that answer.

"Maybe," he tried again, "it's because this is the first five minutes we've been together that we weren't frantic about something or other. I find myself almost uncontrollably attracted to you, and I'm just doing what I naturally do when I'm in that state."

"Coming on."

"If you want to call it that. Don't tell me you don't feel it too. I haven't forgotten that kiss."

She blushed to the tips of her ears. "So, I kissed you."

"So, I played with your hair. You wanted an explanation. You got it." He fell silent, crossing his forearms in front of him and resting his cheek against them, so he didn't have to look at her. He was such a liar. He could only hope that he'd made her mad enough with his flip lines that she'd leave it alone. Because if she gave him even the slightest encouragement, he was a goner.

He wasn't supposed to touch her. To do so could bring disastrous results. Not only was it reprehensible of him to sleep with his hostage—his former hostage, he reminded himself—it was also dangerous. He didn't need the distraction.

Why had he touched her damn hair, anyway?

"Clint?"

"Yes?" He replied without even raising his head. If he looked into her eyes, he'd be lost.

"Is what we're doing tonight really dangerous? I mean, could we be killed?"

"I haven't decided whether to let you go or not. And yes, we could be shot down like stray dogs in a ghetto if Eddie finds us there. I do not underestimate the man's ruthlessness, especially now that the net is closing in on him."

"Then maybe we should go to the authorities."

"I *am* the authorities."

"Oh, Clint, I'm not an idiot. Your superior has no idea what you're doing, and he wouldn't allow it if he knew."

"That's why we can't go to him. If Neil McCormick found out that I'd compromised this investigation, the best we could hope for is that he would order the arrests of everyone we have the goods on so far—including Jimmy. We'd get a search warrant for the Foxhunt. And the Big Boss, the one we really want, would slither out of sight. He'd find another pipeline onto the streets."

"So instead you're going to risk your life."

"It's a calculated risk. And it's not illegal. Jimmy technically owns that club, and he can let in anybody he wants."

"What do you hope to find?"

"A name, a phone number, a bank account—something that will lead me to the man I'm looking for."

Marissa paused, then declared, "I'm going with you."

"Marissa—"

"Three of us can search faster than two. We'll get in and out quicker that way. Please, Clint. I don't think I could stand staying behind, waiting, not knowing if you're okay."

"Gee, honey, I didn't know you cared," he quipped.

"Well, I do, dammit. Don't ask me why."

The catch in her voice moved him as nothing else could have. She was right, there was no reason for her to care. But she obviously did.

Clint raised his head. She was looking at him, her dark eyes telltale shiny. Something lodged in his throat. He couldn't stop looking at her, drinking in the emotion he saw reflected on her face. She seemed to have stopped breathing. So had he.

To hell with it. He leaned forward, grabbed a handful of that magnificent, tangled hair, and kissed her.

The first contact was explosive. The entirety of Clint's consciousness focused on the feel of her soft, responsive lips against his—and his reaction, lower down in his body.

Marissa suddenly broke the kiss and rolled over onto her back, off the pillow. She was almost gasping for air, her unbound breasts rising and falling beneath the cranberry shirt. Her nipples, which had barely shown through before, were straining against the soft cotton in rigid peaks. "Clint . . ."

He tossed the pillow out of the way. His skin was on fire; his hands itched to touch those breasts. He moved in closer, ready to reclaim the embrace, ready to soothe away any objections she might have.

He didn't have to. Whatever she'd been about to say, she decided against it. In a move that took his breath away, she reached behind his neck and pulled him down to her. The next thing he knew he was lying on top of her, his hands buried in her hair, his legs tangled with hers.

His arousal pressed against her belly. She had to feel it, had to know how little control he really had right now. But she showed no hesitation. Her hands were under his shirt, lightly raking the bare skin of his back with her nails. Her hips wiggled provocatively against him, driving him insane.

Worried that he would crush her, he rolled over onto his back, pulling her with him. Other than to quickly move her hands to his chest, she didn't even break rhythm. Though his own brain was in a fog of thick and murky desire, he was still aware enough to realize that if one of them didn't do something, clothes were going to fly, and he would make love to Marissa Gabriole right there on the living room floor—with her brother sleeping upstairs.

He tried to make himself stop kissing her, but he couldn't.

Finally it was Marissa who broke the kiss. She slumped against him, panting. "You son of a—"

"Pardon?" What the hell had he done now?

"How could you do this to me?"

"I haven't done anything . . . yet."

"You made me want you. You're impossible. You represent everything I despise—violence and crime and things nice people don't talk about." There was no animosity in her voice, only frustration. "I haven't rolled around on the floor with a boy since I was seventeen."

"I'm not a boy." Even if he was acting like a hormone-driven teenager.

"I noticed. And I'm not seventeen. But we can't have sex right here with my brother sleeping upstairs."

Surprised by his own burst of energy, Clint was on his feet in seconds, dragging Marissa with him. "If *that*'s your only objection. . . ."

"Where are we going?" But she didn't balk as he led her through the living room, dining room, and kitchen. Off the kitchen there was a laundry room with a door. And a lock.

Giving her little chance to object, he closed and locked the door. Light from one tiny window illuminated the closet-sized room, but barely. Marissa's eyes grew wide as he backed her up against the wall and yanked the hem of her shirt from her jeans. "I'm going to make love to you. Now. I'm not usually this pushy, but I don't know when or if we'll ever get another chance. Things are going to move pretty quickly after tonight. I'll either be in jail or in hiding."

As he made this speech—a cohesive collection of

thoughts, considering the state he was in—he'd reached under her shirt to caress her breasts. They were incredibly warm and soft.

She closed her eyes and threw her head back. An uninterpretable sound came from her throat.

With his last bit of conscience, he said, "If you have any objections, make them now."

She shook her head.

"Then please tell me you're on the pill," he said, almost desperate. " 'Cause I sure as hell don't have anything here."

She shook her head. "I don't care."

Well, he did, dammit. He wanted to leave Marissa with memories, not a baby. Why did he suddenly have to develop scruples?

She whipped her shirt over her head, revealing her creamy breasts to his hungry eyes.

"Oh, Marissa." She was pulling out all the stops. No fair.

Next she shimmied out of her jeans and panties in one movement. "C'mon, Ace," she taunted him. "You started this thing. Finish it." She took his hand and guided it to the gently swelling mound at the apex of her thighs. She quivered at his first touch to the silky curls that shrouded her femininity, then whimpered as he slid his fingers between her warm folds.

Clint closed his eyes and held on to the edge of the washing machine, afraid his knees would buckle, as he reveled in the intimate caress.

She climaxed in seconds, muffling her cries of ecstasy

against his shoulder. Then she slumped against him, crying in earnest. "I'm sorry, Clint."

He was astounded—by her passion, by her reaction to it. *Sorry?* "For what?"

"For being crazy. I'm sure all this is your fault somehow, but I still feel guilty. You don't even have your clothes off."

"I can fix that." She didn't have to ask him twice. He ripped his shirt off over his head. Seconds later he'd shucked his jeans. Marissa's hands never left him as he undressed. They caressed and explored, leaving trails of heat wherever they went.

When she touched his arousal with a hint of shyness, he thought he would jump out of his skin with the intensity of his pleasure.

"Marissa, if you keep doing that—"

"I know perfectly well what will happen." Then she leaned into him, pressing her belly against him. "I want to take you inside me," she whispered. "Please, don't pick now to start acting like a gentleman."

He knew it was wrong; he knew it was crazy. But he could no more stop what happened next than he could have stopped the storm that sank their boat. He braced himself against the locked door, grasped Marissa's hips, and lifted her those few extra inches she needed to become one with him.

She sighed, then gasped as he slowly lowered her onto his rigid arousal. He couldn't help gasping himself. Right or wrong, nothing in his life had ever felt so good. Marissa clasped her legs around his hips and her arms around his neck.

He didn't have to do a damn thing. With seeming effortlessness, Marissa moved her body against his by mere fractions of an inch. But that was all he needed. He held on for as long as he could, wanting to extend her pleasure, but he was so wound up that his best effort at self-control wasn't much. In what seemed far too short a time, he exploded within her and damn near passed out from the sheer expenditure of energy.

Amazingly, Marissa climaxed again, shuddering as if she'd caught a fatal fever.

Maybe she had.

As Clint regained his senses, he realized how uncomfortable Marissa must be. He bent his knees and lowered her until her feet touched the floor, then gently disengaged himself from her.

"Did we just make love in a laundry room?" she asked breathlessly, still clinging to him.

"Yeah. It wasn't bad."

"Aw, c'mon, Clint, you can do better than that."

"It was the main highlight of my life so far, okay?" He softened the jibe by smoothing her hair from her face. He didn't mean to be flip. This *was* something he'd never forget. But what could he say in such a situation? Undying love would be in poor taste, considering they were as mismatched a pair as any two people he could think of. A Mafia princess and a burned-out, rogue FBI agent. He wanted to put her brother in jail, and she probably would prefer it if he'd drowned the previous night. It would have saved her a lot of grief.

"That's an improvement. Think how much better it would be in a king-size bed."

Aw, hell. That wasn't going to happen, nice as it sounded. As soon as he turned over his evidence to Neil, he would be gone from Marissa's life one way or another. He decided not to take her up on her invitation to think about anything, but especially about a repeat of their recent performance.

"We better get cleaned up," he said gruffly.

Marissa immediately pulled away, suddenly all business. "Right. Jimmy will be up and around anytime." She busied herself searching for her hastily discarded clothes.

Clint was wishing he could see her face. Had he hurt her feelings? That wasn't what he'd meant. He had a genuine fondness for the woman. No, it was more than fondness. An attachment. An illogical connection to her, given they'd known each other less than twenty-four hours. But he realized, perhaps better than she did, how disastrous, if not downright impossible, a relationship between them would be. He represented everything she'd spent her whole life trying to escape, deny, and when denying wasn't possible, despise.

He was a lowlife, married to the Bureau and his damnable job more securely than he'd ever been bound to Rachelle. There was no way to separate who he was from what he'd done, what he continued to do.

He wasn't the man for Marissa, and the sooner she reached that conclusion, the better.

As Marissa hastily dressed, the enormity of what she and Clint had done came home to her. Rutting in the laundry room like a couple of animals in heat! What insanity had come over her?

But, oh, how sweet it had been. For those few blissful minutes, she and Clint had been one in mind, body, and spirit. At least that's the way it had felt to her. She suspected Clint felt different, given his current mood. Any fool could see that this soul-stirring experience had been nothing more than a lark for him, a tension reliever.

She tried not to feel slighted. He was a guy, after all. There had been no promises between them, only white-hot need that refused to be denied. She would count herself lucky to have experienced Clint's lovemaking and move on.

Yeah, right, she thought as she tucked in her shirt. Right now, with her body thrumming with satisfaction, she couldn't imagine a single second of her life going by that she wouldn't relive and relish those few minutes she'd spent in a strange laundry room with a renegade lover. Nothing in her conservative experience had prepared her for such an event, and she doubted anything in her future would, either.

"You ready?" Clint asked.

"Ready as I'll ever be." She wished he would kiss her. Just one last kiss, a sort of punctuation mark to their escapade. But he seemed to have forgotten his ardent affection for her. He cracked open the laundry room door. "Coast is clear."

"Great. I have dibs on the shower." She slipped past him with her head held high, hoping she could get out of his sight before she gave in to what she was *really* feeling.

She did. She held herself together until she was in the

shower upstairs, letting the needles of steaming water pour down on her. Then she gave in to a few quiet sobs.

Why had she done it? She hadn't accomplished anything except to give herself a taste of something she couldn't have again. She hadn't even used birth control. Oh, God, what if she was pregnant?

The chances were negligible, she told herself. Why worry about it? She would cross that bridge when and if she had to.

Still, an insidious little voice inside her mentioned that it wouldn't be so bad to bear Clint Nichols's child. They would share a lifelong bond, even if he could never bring himself to love her.

Love her? Is that what she was hoping for? Ridiculous. What would she do with someone like him, except worry every night about whether he would come home?

She scrubbed relentlessly with the sliver of strong soap she found in the shower until she was sure every last molecule of Clint was removed from her body. Feeling stronger and much more pragmatic, she turned off the flow of water, dried herself off, and climbed back into her borrowed clothes.

She encountered Clint at the top of the stairs. "Bathroom's all yours," she said, not looking at him.

He didn't let her get away with that. He snagged her arm and twirled her around as she was about to put her foot on the top stair. She couldn't help but look at him. There was something compelling in his thundercloud gaze, something she couldn't put a name to.

He captured her lips with his, then quickly released

her. "You really are something special, Marissa," he said, his voice sounding thick.

Too stunned to respond, she stared as he turned his back and went into the bathroom.

Four o'clock in the morning was damnably early, Marissa decided as she stood arguing with Clint in the kitchen while they both downed some hot coffee out of paper cups.

"For the last time, you're not coming with us to the Foxhunt," Clint said in an annoyingly even tone.

"Yes, I am," Marissa said just as calmly. "If you leave me behind, I will call the FBI the minute you leave, and I'll get hold of your boss, and I'll tell him everything."

"Hah! Call the FBI on what? You won't have a phone."

"I'll go find a phone."

"You don't have a car."

"I'll walk."

They stared at each other. Marissa had a feeling Clint was only posturing. She knew she was. No matter how angry she was at being excluded, she wouldn't blow the whole operation by contacting the authorities. She'd get both Clint and Jimmy arrested and/or killed. Clint probably knew that.

Still, his infuriation with her was obvious. "I'll tie you up before we leave," he said, upping the stakes.

"Hey, hey, hey," Jimmy broke in. "I don't want to hear none of that, Nichols. I'd already like to flatten your nose for what you did to my sister last night, and I won't stand by and let you manhandle her again."

Marissa stifled a smile. If only Jimmy knew exactly how Clint had manhandled her that afternoon.

"Look, it's not that dangerous," Jimmy reasoned, reversing his earlier stand. "The place closes at two, and it's a tomb by two-thirty. There's no reason for anyone to be there at four in the morning. Deliveries don't start arriving till after six."

She could see the indecision in Clint's eyes, a tiny chink in his armor. She intended to make the best of it. No way was she letting Clint or Jimmy out of her sight until Eddie Constantine was safely behind bars. "You can use a third person," she reasoned. "You'll get done quicker if I'm there to help. My eyes are fresh. I don't have the same prejudices going in as you or Jimmy do."

"No," Clint said.

Marissa pulled out the big guns. "Well, see if I ever save your miserable life again not once but twice."

"And I'm still trying to figure out why you did it," Jimmy grumbled.

"Oh, all right, fine," Clint said. Marissa suspected that if he really thought they would be in danger, he wouldn't have given in. He was one stubborn honcho. Then again, she was beginning to see that she had a certain way with him. She was something more than a hunk of female flesh to him, though how much more she couldn't begin to guess.

The forty-five-minute drive to the Foxhunt proceeded in sullen silence, with Clint at the wheel of Jimmy's car. He spoke up only when they neared their destination, and only, Marissa suspected, because he felt he had to.

"Jimmy, you're the only one of us who could conceivably have legitimate business at the club," he began. "I'd like you to be our lookout. If anyone shows up, give us a signal and run interference. Do you have a cover story as to why you might be there this time of night?"

"Uh . . ." Jimmy came up blank.

"How about you wanted to count the cash receipts?" Marissa suggested.

Jimmy shook his head. "That wouldn't work. I don't even have access to the cash register. I'm pretty much a figurehead, you know. I may own the place, but Eddie runs it. He pays me a salary—in cash—and I don't worry about the business end."

"Jimmy!" Marissa scolded him. "That's reprehensible. You mean to tell me all those figures you supplied for your tax return were a total lie? I could go to jail right along with you for preparing that return!"

"I know, I know. I shouldn't have involved you, but my bookkeeper quit—"

"Can we save this for later?" Clint interrupted. "Jimmy, you need a cover story. How about you had a rendezvous with one of the dancers after work, but she stood you up?"

"What? Are you kidding? Sophia would have my—"

"You're not really going to do it, Jimmy," Marissa reminded him. "Just say you are. Lord knows you weren't faithful to your first two wives. No one would even blink."

"Hey, hey, that's not nice, sissy."

"I calls 'em like I sees 'em," she said.

"All right," Jimmy said. "As a cover story, that stinks, but there won't be nobody there anyway. If you two are going to do the searching, though, let me give you some ideas on where to start. Eddie has more hidey-holes than a squirrel."

"Okay." Clint pulled into the driveway of a huge, garish pink stucco building. The neon signs were turned off, but Marissa could easily read them in the city light. " 'The Foxhunt. Hottest girls in town'?" she read aloud. " 'Triple X'? Some English pub."

"Sorry, sis," Jimmy mumbled as Clint pulled the car around back, where it couldn't be seen from the street. "But you would have freaked if I told you the truth."

"No kidding." She shook her head. Her own brother, a purveyor of smut.

"It's a classy place," Jimmy said. "Our girls always wear—"

"Please, I don't want to hear it."

Jimmy unlocked the back door. He punched in a series of numbers on the security alarm's keypad. As soon as everyone was safely inside, he locked the door and punched some more keys. "I'm setting the alarm so no one can sneak up on us," he said. "It'll beep inside all the offices if anyone goes in or out."

Marissa followed the two men inside, staring in frank fascination at the autographed pictures that lined the hallway leading back to the offices. "Chesty Drawers?" she read, incredulous. "How forward-thinking of her parents to give her a name so suitable to her looks and profession."

The men made no reply. They seemed to be en-
grossed in unlocking the door to one of the offices. Burning with curiosity, Marissa wandered back down the
hallway and into the club itself. She paused before a six-
foot poster of a woman she presumed was the current star
attraction. The photograph left little to the imagination.
Marissa felt her face heating up.

Suddenly Clint appeared by her side, grabbing her
arm. "Don't wander away like that! You said you wanted
to help, so let's get to work. We'll start in Eddie's office. I
don't suppose you're any good at cracking safes."

When they entered Eddie's inner sanctum, an opu-
lently appointed office with artistically arranged nude
sculptures and paintings everywhere, Marissa saw immediately why Clint had asked her that question. A safe with
a key lock sat atop the filing cabinet. "Darn. If he's got
anything worth finding, it's in that safe. We might as well
go home." She was starting to feel creepy anyway.

"Not yet. Jimmy told me that when this place was
being built, he remembers some sort of chamber being
put in beneath the floor here. Eddie told him he'd
planned to put a safe there, then changed his mind. Let's
see if that's really the case. Help me move this desk."

"Shouldn't we be wearing gloves or something?
We're leaving prints all over the place!" Marissa asked as
she took hold of one end of the massive mahogany desk
and heaved. It took several tries before they were able to
scoot it off the oriental carpet. Marissa leaned against a
sculpture, realized what she was touching, and jumped
back.

"We're completely within our legal rights," Clint reminded her. "Jimmy owns the place, and he let us in and gave us permission to search. Don't worry about it."

Yeah. As if she wasn't going to worry. She was worried about everything, including why Clint had been treating her like a stranger since that last, hurried kiss at the top of the stairs. She knew he was preoccupied with this mission, but—

"Help me roll up this rug," he ordered her.

She saluted crisply. "Yes sir."

"You said you wanted to help, so help."

"Man, you get testy when you're stressed." She started rolling the carpet from her end. When the floor was cleared, she stared at it, trying to make out any tell-tale seams or cracks in the gleaming hardwood.

Clint pulled out a pocket knife and started testing the seams one by one. "This might take a while. You could start going through the desk, but make sure you leave everything the way you found it."

"Okay." She'd wanted to be useful. Here was her chance.

The desk proved to be a hodgepodge of invoices, receipts, checkbooks, pink message slips, business cards— any one of which could lead Clint to the Big Boss. If she'd had something to write with . . .

Then she spied the copy machine in the corner of the office. Quickly she gathered up the message slips, trying to remember the approximate location of each before she removed it.

Clint looked up when the copy machine came to life. "What are you doing?"

"Copying stuff so you can look at it later. These

names don't mean anything to me, but maybe they'll help."

"That's a good idea. Copy anything you can drag over there."

She did just that, systematically copying every piece of paper she could find, then artistically re-creating the original chaos when she was done.

"How about check stubs?"

"Yeah, great. You never know. He could be—" Clint fell suddenly silent.

"He could be what? Clint?" Marissa stopped what she was doing and looked over. He was staring. Concerned that something was wrong, she walked to the other side of the desk, which blocked her vision. Then she saw what had reduced him to silence.

Money. Cash, great gobs of it in a compartment beneath the floor. Stacks and stacks of bound bills. "Omigosh," she shrieked. "How much is there?"

"I don't know," Clint said. "There must be at least a million dollars here. There are only a couple of reasons he would stockpile cash like this, neatly counted and bound. Either he's planning to buy a one-way ticket to Argentina, or he's getting ready to make a record-setting buy. I'm banking on the latter."

"What are you going to do? Is this the evidence you need? Can you call your boss now?"

Clint sat back on his haunches. "No. What we need to know is when and where. And ten to one what we need is in that damn safe." He pawed through the stacks of green. "There's nothing here but the money."

Marissa watched, fascinated, as he took a tiny camera

out of his shirt pocket and photographed the money from every imaginable angle. "Another fibbie toy?" she asked.

"Nope. This one's my own personal toy. I bought it out of the back of a magazine when I was twelve. Best twenty-two bucks I ever spent."

She fidgeted as he took his time over the photos. They'd been there over an hour now. Jimmy swore nobody showed up till daylight, but what did he know? He probably wasn't ever there at this time.

Finally Clint finished. She helped him with the rug, then the desk. They spent another few minutes riffling through the file cabinet, but it appeared Eddie wasn't the type to keep his files neat and up-to-date. Nothing piqued Clint's interest.

"Well, I guess that about does—" He stopped. "What was that?"

"What?" Marissa barely breathed the word. Then she heard it—voices.

TEN

"What the hell?" Clint said under his breath. "Jimmy was supposed to let us know if someone was coming."

"Maybe someone took him by surprise," Marissa whispered back. She clutched her thick stack of photocopies to her chest. "Let's get out of here. It sounds as though whoever is here came through the front."

Clint did a visual sweep of the office. Everything looked pretty much as they'd found it. He turned out the lights and locked the door behind him, leaving himself and Marissa in the dim corridor.

He could hear the voices more plainly now. Two men, one of them Jimmy. If that weasel had betrayed him, Clint would—

"They're getting closer," Marissa hissed. "They're coming this way. I think it's Eddie."

They both took off at a dead run for the back exit. But Jimmy had locked the door and reset the alarm when they'd entered. Clint grabbed Marissa's arm just as she reached for the door. "We can't get out this way. We'll set off the alarm, and that could put Jimmy in danger."

"What then?" Marissa looked up at him, her eyes wide with panic, expecting him to come up with a solution.

He did his best. "This way." He recalled seeing a maintenance closet across from Eddie's office. He found it, opened the door, pushed Marissa inside, and followed. He got the door closed just as the two men rounded the corner.

"I knew you'd come around sooner or later," one man was saying—the one who wasn't Jimmy. "You can't let a woman totally monopolize you the way Sophia does. It makes a man weak. Having some affairs—it's the best thing you can do for a marriage. Make sure she knows about it too. It'll keep her in line, make her realize she's expendable."

Clint pulled Marissa close. "Eddie?" he whispered.

"Yes," she whispered back, clutching her stack of photocopies to her chest. "Oh, God, Clint, we're in trouble."

"Shh. There's no reason he'd come in here."

Jimmy was responding to Eddie's advice. "Hey, hey, now, don't you go telling Sophia anything. I love that woman."

"Of course you do, buddy. She's a peach. We *all* love Sophia, if you get my drift."

"What are you trying to say?"

"Just that a leopard doesn't change her spots, Jimmy. I knew her before you did, don't forget."

"Knew her how?" Jimmy roared.

Oh, for God's sake, Clint thought, this was no time

for Jimmy to get into a pissing match over a woman. Why didn't they go into Eddie's office instead of standing out there in the hall acting like a couple of teenagers fighting over a cheerleader?

Marissa shifted her weight, leaning up against him. "Sorry," she whispered. "It's kinda crowded in here—ooh!" The last part came out as a clearly audible yelp.

Clint swung his arm around her and placed his hand over her mouth. "Shhhh. Do you want to die?"

She shook her head, and he released her. "Something crawled over my foot." She barely breathed the words.

"What was that?" Eddie asked.

"What? I didn't hear nothing," Jimmy said.

Marissa grabbed Clint's hand and squeezed. "I'm scared."

"So am I." He squeezed back.

"Why do you keep looking at the closet?" Eddie demanded.

Clint held his breath, wanting very badly to curse. They were goners, and all because Jimmy was a rotten liar. How could he ever have believed Jimmy Gabriole was the mastermind behind an ingenious drug business?

"Marissa?" he whispered, his mouth close to her ear. "What?"

"For what it's worth, I've been trying very hard not to fall in love with you."

She gasped, and he took the opportunity to kiss her. If they were going to die in a broom closet, he wanted to go with a smile on his face. Marissa melted against him. He savored the taste of her for one last second, then got his mind back on business.

They needed weapons. He handed Marissa a mop. "When that door opens, hit anything that moves." For himself, he got a bottle of glass cleaner and a toilet plunger.

"Jimmy, who've you got in that closet?" Eddie asked in a deathly calm voice.

"Nobody, Eddie, I swear it."

"Then you wouldn't mind if I sprayed that closet door with bullets—"

"No! Eddie, stop, please. There's a . . . a woman in there!"

Clint braced himself for the barrage of bullets. It didn't come. Instead, the closet door was yanked open. Clint sprayed a stream of glass cleaner in Eddie's face while Marissa wielded the mop as if she were a samurai warrior with a sword.

Clint didn't even get to use the plunger. Eddie crumpled to the ground.

"God Almighty, that's the second person I've bashed over the head in twenty-four hours," said a stunned Marissa. "I've turned into a cavewoman."

"Oh, Jeez," Jimmy was saying. "I'm a dead man."

"You did the best you could," Clint said, feeling surprisingly detached now that the crisis was over. He divested Eddie of his gun, then checked his pulse. "Nice job, Marissa. He's out cold, but he's plenty alive."

"That's not funny! I could have killed him."

"He was gonna kill you, sis," Jimmy pointed out. "He would've, too, if I hadn't stopped him. He'd have filled that closet full of lead and asked questions later. The fact that he don't like killing women is the only thing that saved your life."

"Let's get out of here, shall we?" Marissa said.

"Wait." Clint started fishing in the pockets of the unconscious man.

"Are you crazy?" Marissa asked. "I want out of here."

Though he hated to, Clint ignored her distress. He'd come here to do a job, and he wasn't leaving until it was done. He came up with a set of keys. "One of these opens that safe."

Marissa immediately changed her tune. "Oh, great idea!"

"Jimmy, you and Marissa watch him. If he so much as twitches, yell." With that, Clint reentered Eddie's office. He found the safe key and put it into the lock. It turned with a satisfying click, and the door swung open.

At first, Clint thought the safe was empty, and his heart sank. Then he saw the small, leather-bound book hiding in a back corner. He took it out and flipped through it. It was a ledger book, with pages and pages of mind-bogglingly huge figures. There were dates, names, and coded words that probably indicated various kinds of illegal contraband.

Clint wanted to take the book with him. But then Eddie would know he'd been found out, and he would fold up his tents and be gone to South America or Switzerland. The success of his investigation depended on Eddie's believing the incriminating evidence in his office was still his secret.

One final notation intrigued him—today's date, a

time, and a location. Would that be the appointment all that cash was destined for?

"Clint!" Marissa called. "He's moving."

Clint committed the notation to memory, shoved the book back into the safe, and shut the door. In seconds he was back in the hallway, replacing the keys in Eddie's pants pocket. The man stirred, opened his eyes.

"Huh?"

"It's a nightmare, Eddie," Clint said, patting the man's cheek. "Go back to sleep."

"Oh, okay." Eddie obediently closed his eyes. The three coconspirators established a new speed record in exiting a building.

"I'm a dead man," Jimmy mumbled over and over even after they'd cleared the parking lot. "I betrayed my best friend."

"Oh, knock it off, Jimmy," Marissa said. "We're all in trouble with Eddie. But in a matter of hours he'll be behind bars. Right, Clint?"

Clint said nothing.

"Right, Clint?" she repeated.

"He's going to make a buy," Clint finally responded. "A huge buy. If he doesn't cancel it after what's happened. If he goes ahead with it—we can get the Big Boss."

"When?" Marissa asked.

"Tonight. I need to talk to McCormick. I'm going to tell him everything, and turn over the evidence I have and hope it's enough. I'll drop you two back at the safe house first."

"I'm coming with you," Marissa announced.

"Where have I heard this before? Absolutely not. It's not necessary to drag you any deeper into this mess."

"Clint, I'm in as deep as I can get. I've assaulted two people. I've stolen things from a man's private office. I've made private use of FBI property—"

"Exactly why you shouldn't go with me."

"You plan to leave me out of the report you give your boss? How are you going to explain how you got the evidence?"

"I'll say I broke in."

"Then you really *will* be arrested. No way. Take me with you to talk to your boss, or I'll go to him on my own."

Clint sighed. The damn woman was driving him nuts. Had he really told her he was falling in love with her? Did she remember?

Was it true?

"I'm coming with you too," Jimmy said.

Clint rolled his eyes. "Oh, hell."

"I'm turning myself in and begging for protective custody. It's the only way I'll stay alive. Eddie won't believe any story I could come up with to explain what happened. He'll kill me, or have me killed."

"But, Jimmy," Marissa protested, "you haven't done anything wrong, not really."

"I haven't killed nobody, and I haven't dealt drugs. But I've done an awful lot of looking the other way."

"Oh, Jimmy," Marissa said on a hopeless sigh.

"I know, sis. I always promised you I wouldn't end up like Dad, but you were just a kid when it happened. I was a grown man. It was Eddie's uncle who done the bombing, you know, and they saw me as a threat. I had to go along with Eddie, whatever he said to do. It was that, or end up as dead as Mom and Dad."

Marissa sobbed, and Clint's heart went out to her. He felt her pain as if it were his own.

"How did you know?" she asked. "About the bomb. Why didn't you tell the police?"

Clint shook his head. She really was an innocent.

"It was Eddie's uncle who took over, that's how I knew who was responsible," Jimmy said. "And the police knew. They also knew better than to point fingers. Back then, they pretty much let the families take care of their own problems."

"It's not too late, you know," Marissa said.

"Too late for what?" Jimmy asked.

"To walk away from it. We could both move away, change our names."

Clint swallowed with a mouth gone suddenly dry. He didn't like thinking about Marissa disappearing from his life. He wanted to know where she was while he did his time.

"Sissy," Jimmy said, "if I get through this alive, and a free man, I'll go anywhere you want to go."

What were the chances of that happening? Clint wondered.

Clint's boss, Neil McCormick, lived in a stately colonial in Bellaire, one of Houston's most elegant neighborhoods. Marissa whistled as Clint pulled in the driveway. "They're paying federal workers okay these days."

"Don't you believe it," Clint said. "Neil inherited some kind of fortune. He makes more than me, but not that much."

Neil himself answered the door, appearing remarkably unsurprised. Though it was only six A.M., he was neatly dressed and groomed. With his small stature, wire-rimmed glasses, and balding pate, he was nothing like Marissa had pictured.

Still, first impressions could be deceiving, she decided as the small man ushered them all inside. Behind the glasses, his eyes were sharp as an eagle's. It wouldn't be easy getting anything past him. Yet that was exactly what she planned to do.

A shiver of apprehension passed through her. If she wasn't careful, she would land all three of them in prison.

Clint introduced Jimmy and Marissa to Neil. The other man showed no surprise beyond a raised eyebrow as he shook hands with both of them. He led them into the living room, which was expensively furnished in leather. Clint hadn't mentioned his boss's marital status, but Marissa was betting he was a bachelor, probably married to his work. So deeply imbedded in that dark, nether-world of crime that he didn't have time for a woman.

Like Clint, she couldn't help thinking.

"Okay, Clint, spill it," McCormick said without preamble when they were all awkwardly seated. "It appears to me you've disobeyed direct orders in a big way. If we can salvage whatever mess you've created, I might see my way clear to letting you retire early." He said all this in a deceptively friendly tone.

Clint didn't even act surprised. "All I want is for this

operation to close successfully. With what I've learned over the past day and a half, I think we can do that."

"You mean *I* can do it," McCormick said. "You're not doing anything pending the outcome of an administrative hearing on your fitness as an FBI agent."

Marissa suddenly found her voice. "I think you're being overly harsh, Mr. McCormick. Clint was trying to save his ex-wife's life, someone you apparently thought wasn't worth saving."

Clint shot her a warning look. "Turns out she wasn't," he said harshly. "Save it, Marissa. I can speak for myself."

"Please, do." McCormick folded his arms and waited.

Clint cleared his throat, but Marissa continued before he could even begin. "He came to me," she said. "Just to talk. He thought I might know something. I knew my brother had nothing to do with Rachelle's disappearance, so I brought Clint and Jimmy together."

Clint and Jimmy stared at her, mouths gaping. Well? What was she supposed to do, tell this man who held Clint's career in his palm that he'd kidnapped her and stolen Jimmy's boat?

"Jimmy was willing to cooperate," she continued. "We found out through Rachelle's brother that she was perfectly fine, and that she and Eddie Constantine had faked her disappearance to lure Clint into the open. So they could kill him."

McCormick's right eyebrow twitched. Marissa couldn't tell whether he was surprised, angry, or amused by her story.

He looked at Clint. "You concur with this?"

"It's mostly true. Jimmy Gabriole isn't the key to this

operation. Constantine set things up to make it look that way, but Gabriole is mostly a puppet."

Marissa thought Jimmy would take umbrage at this summation, but instead he was nodding eagerly. "Yeah, that's right," he said. "A puppet. And now Eddie wants to kill me, too, or he will when he wakes up."

"Excuse me?" McCormick said.

Clint took over the story from there. He told his boss about searching Eddie's office, and their confrontation with the man himself. When he got to the part about the secret ledger book in the safe, McCormick finally appeared impressed.

"Tonight?" he said excitedly. "The buy is going down tonight?"

"At eleven," Clint said.

"Wait a minute. If he saw you there, won't Constantine call it off? He'll know he's been compromised."

"He doesn't know that I looked in the safe, or that I found his hidey-hole in the floor. I'm not sure he even knows I was there. All he knows is that he opened a broom closet and got assaulted."

McCormick groaned. "You didn't hurt him bad, did you? All I need is for this to make the papers."

"I'm the one who hit him," Marissa volunteered. Clint was in enough trouble.

"He had a gun in his hand," Jimmy added. "It was purely self-defense."

"Yeah, yeah." McCormick waved away Jimmy's explanation. "Let's skip over that part. How're we going to explain, in court, how you got this information? Stealing an unconscious man's keys doesn't cut it."

"The information could have been lying out in the open," Clint said.

"But it wasn't!"

"So what, are you going to sit on the one chance we'll ever get to nail this bastard because of a little snafu in procedure? We'll let the lawyers figure out that part. Let's just put together a welcome wagon."

McCormick sighed. "All right. What, exactly, do you expect me to do with these two?" He gestured toward the Gabrioles.

"Arrest me, for God's sake," Jimmy said. "I'll cooperate a hundred percent. I know lots of stuff. Just protect me until Eddie's arrested. He'll kill me otherwise."

"Yeah, I guess that's the thing to do." McCormick turned to Marissa. "What about you?"

"Arrest her too," Clint said.

"What?" Marissa stared at him, at a total loss. He was turning on her, after everything she'd done to help him?

"What charge?" McCormick asked.

"Assault. She tried to shoot me."

Marissa went weak. He was right. She'd shot at Clint, hit Rusty over the head with a lamp, and assaulted Eddie with a mop. She belonged someplace where she couldn't hurt anybody.

"Okay." McCormick stood. "I think jail's the safest place for all of you. What do you say we all take a little trip downtown?"

During the drive to Bureau headquarters in McCormick's Infiniti, Marissa alternated between steaming at

Clint and feeling sorry for herself. He really was a beast, to make love with her and then toss her away, now that she'd outlived her usefulness. He hadn't even spared her a glance. And what was that business about falling in love with her? He'd said something to that effect when they thought they were seconds away from turning into Swiss cheese. What had been his motive?

She'd brought this on herself, she supposed. The minute she threw in her lot with the devil, she'd sealed her fate. Putting Eddie in jail—that was the important thing. And keeping Jimmy safe. She could only hope that Clint would keep his promise to put in a good word for her brother.

A reception committee was waiting for them in the underground parking garage below the FBI building. Two anonymous-looking men ushered her and Jimmy onto an elevator. McCormick and Clint went in the opposite direction, with no good-bye, thanks, good luck on your trip up the river.

Now Marissa wasn't simply steamed, she was boiling. This was the last time she stuck out her neck for any man. And the next time one of that despicable sex told her she was free to walk away, she was damn sure going to do it!

On the third floor, the two silent guards showed her and Jimmy to a room sparsely furnished with some plastic chairs, a table, and a tiny refrigerator. They were locked into the room without explanation.

"I think this is illegal," Marissa said.

"I don't care, sis," Jimmy said, collapsing into one of the chairs. He looked like a man who'd been relieved of a tremendous burden. "It feels safe. You know, I haven't felt safe in twenty years."

"I wish you'd talked to me about what was going on," she said. She opened the fridge and found some cold soda. "Maybe I could have helped. We could have figured some way out."

He shook his head. "I guess I didn't really want out bad enough. Getting money for nothing is kind of addictive after a while."

She popped the top on her soda can, handed it to him, and got herself another. "Do you think we'll go to jail?"

"I don't know about you, but the minute I get to a phone, I'm calling a lawyer. I figure I can trade what I know, or what they think I know, for some kind of immunity. You, they're not serious about putting you in jail. That's just Clint, keeping you safe the only way he knows how."

"Keeping me out of the way, you mean."

"No, keeping you safe. I've seen how he looks at you, and don't think I haven't wanted to punch him out for that as much as anything."

Clint was royally pissed off. He'd spent the last four and a half hours with Neil and the rest of the task force—FBI, DEA, SWAT team, local law enforcement—going over every minute detail of what he'd learned. Neil had not so subtly hinted that he was in a lot of trouble, and nothing short of complete cooperation would keep him on the payroll.

Not that it mattered so much to him anymore. Get-

ting fired was the least of his worries. It was Marissa he
agonized over. Neil wouldn't tell him where she was,
wouldn't even assure him she was safe.

The woman was incredible. She'd sat there on Neil's
couch while the man glowered at her, calmly lying
through her teeth about how she'd gotten involved in this
mess—all for him. There'd been no mention of hijacking
or boat sinking or guns and knives, not even a breath
about the unauthorized use of government property.
She'd even taken total responsibility for assaulting Eddie.

He found his mind straying in her direction even as
the task force planned their crucial operation for that
night. He couldn't deny that he felt something for her,
something powerful. He'd never met a woman anything
like her—smart, strong, capable, funny . . . sexy. He
would never forget a certain encounter in a laundry room,
or the way she'd kissed him in that closet when they
thought they were taking their last few breaths.

He'd said something to her then. He couldn't remember his exact words, but he'd felt a wave of emotion so
overwhelming that he'd been forced to articulate it. He
wondered now what he'd declared, and whether she'd
understood or taken him seriously.

He hoped she hadn't heard him. It would save him the
embarrassment of having to take back the words. He
never should have allowed himself to fall apart the way he
had.

Not that he hadn't been sincere. But, come on, who
was he kidding? He and Marissa might share an incredible physical bond, fueled by adrenaline and desperation,
but they had little else in common. She despised what he

did for a living, and what he did for a living defined who he was. She was truth and light and everything that was good. And he'd been living in the shadows too long to come out into the daylight.

"I hope I don't have to say this, but I will anyway," Neil was droning on. "I don't want any heroics. If every man sticks to his job, there's no way these guys can get away. Every avenue of escape will be closed off. We've waited a long time for this, and I don't want anyone getting impatient. I firmly believe we can succeed with this operation without firing a shot."

Clint bit his tongue. Neil had been sitting behind a desk for too long. Eddie Constantine and whomever he did business with would never simply drop their weapons and come peacefully.

"Are there any questions so far?" Neil asked. No one said anything. "Then, can I have volunteers for team one? I'm sure you all realize that the men on team one will be at the greatest risk—"

Clint raised his hand.

Neil looked at him. "I've got a special assignment in mind for you, Nichols. Something you're uniquely qualified to do."

A second man volunteered, then a third. Neil busied himself with coordinating the various assignments, making sure each team was a compatible mix of personalities and abilities. Meanwhile, Clint cooled his heels. He didn't like the sound of this "special assignment."

The task force was dismissed. They all got up, talking nervously, jumping with anticipation.

Clint remained seated, arms folded. "All right, Neil,"

he said when the room cleared and only the two men remained. "What is it you want from me?"

"I need you to take care of the girl."

"The—Marissa?"

"I can't arrest her. She hasn't done anything wrong that I can tell, and I'm already pushing the boundaries by keeping her detained without a good reason. Gabriole's been booked on enough charges to keep him locked up for years. I've asked that he be put in an isolation cell for the time being. But I can't do anything about the sister. You're the only one—"

Clint let loose a string of curses. "You gotta be kidding!"

"Not at all. As I was saying, you're the only one—"

"I've been in on this operation since the beginning. I was the one who started it. You're telling me I can't be in on the bust?"

Neil shook his head. "I'm sorry, Clint. But you're a loose cannon. You've disobeyed orders, you've gone out on your own, a one-man mission. Do I have to tell you that operations like this depend on teamwork? Not only are you suffering from a hero complex, but you're way too emotionally tangled up in this case, what with your ex-wife's involvement."

Clint couldn't believe this was happening to him. But it was, and no amount of arguing was going to change his implacable boss's mind. "Fine," he said hotly. "What am I supposed to do to Marissa?"

"Watch her. She knows you, trusts you. Keep her from going home, and keep her off the phone."

"What, you think she'd betray us?"

"She's one of them," Neil said. "Of course she's co-operating while we're looking. You came to her. What was she supposed to do? But left to her own devices, who knows what she'll do? Her conscience might start bothering her. She could call Constantine, warn him."

Clint thought that was the most patently ridiculous worry he'd ever heard of. Neil was inventing something to keep Clint busy. Well, it wasn't going to work. They weren't going to cut him out of the final act, deny him the pleasure of seeing the look on Constantine's face when it all fell down around his shoulders.

"Sure, all right. I'll watch Marissa."

"Tell her you've been assigned to protect her. Take her to a hotel. Buy her a nice dinner. The Bureau will pick up the tab."

Clint had to admit that if he was being shuffled off the scene, he could do worse than spending the night in a hotel with Marissa. Any other time, under any other circumstances . . .

"Yeah, all right. Where is she?" He'd tuck her safely away in a hotel room and make up some excuse to leave. Then he'd be ready to kick butt.

ELEVEN

Marissa was on her fourth cola, and the caffeine wasn't helping a whole lot. But what else did she have to do in this beastly, empty room where the FBI goons had stashed her?

They'd taken Jimmy away hours earlier. She suspected he was under arrest, but that was what he'd wanted, so she tried not to hurt for him. Her brother had surprised her over the past twenty-four hours. He was more deeply involved in Eddie's criminal activities than she'd ever guessed, and that was a huge disappointment. But he'd also shown surprising flashes of strength. She was especially proud of the fact that he hadn't contradicted the bold-faced lies she'd told, though he was probably itching to let someone know Clint had stolen his boat.

He'd done it for her, because he'd known she wanted to keep Clint out of trouble. Perhaps he even suspected the depth of her feelings for the renegade FBI agent.

Whatever his reasons, she appreciated it. She could only hope he would stick to his story when they interrogated him.

The doorknob rattled, and Marissa prepared herself. No matter which anonymous, unsmiling goon they sent in this time, she was going to give him a piece of her mind. Perhaps a few threats about violating her constitutional rights—which clearly they were doing—would light a fire under someone.

The door opened, and Marissa was on her feet. "It's about—" The words stalled in her throat. Clint.

"Hi, Marissa. Are you okay?"

All the outrage she'd been feeling gurgled and swirled and coalesced into a blazing lightning bolt of anger. "Of course I'm not okay! I've been imprisoned in this stinking room for hours without benefit of a lawyer or a phone call—"

Clint held up his hand to halt her tirade. "Easy, easy. This isn't prison, it's protective custody. You could be in a lot of danger."

"Yeah, well, it *feels* like prison. How long are they going to keep me here?"

"You're free to go."

A sense of relief washed over Marissa, followed by a keen disappointment. Was this it, then? Did she simply walk out and never see Clint again? She'd spent hours convincing herself that there was nothing between her and Clint, that the incredible sex they'd shared was nothing more than a natural, delayed reaction to the stress they'd been under and the close quarters they'd been keeping. She'd even told herself she might never lay eyes on him again—and that she didn't care.

Of course she did care; that's what made this business so humiliating. Whether she wanted it or not, her idiot heart was way involved. She was crazy for Clint Nichols, not that he deserved one minute of her devotion for all the misery he'd brought her. Never mind those thirty minutes of bliss.

"There's a catch, though," Clint said. His mouth was hooked in a half smile, making her wonder what he had up his sleeve. Would he ever play straight with her?

"You can't go home, and you can't contact anyone."

"Some freedom! What am I supposed to do, live on the street? I don't have my purse or my car or—"

"You can come with me. I'm authorized to put you up in a hotel, feed you, and provide you with anything you need for the next twelve hours. By then, Eddie and his friends should be in custody."

For a moment, her interest in bringing Eddie down outweighed her indignation. "How's it going to happen? Will you get the Big Boss too?"

Clint was annoyingly silent.

"Oh, I get it. Confidential information. Now that I've served my purpose, I'm out of the loop, I guess."

He shrugged.

"What if I don't want to cooperate?"

He shrugged again. "It means the Bureau will waste a lot of time and manpower following you around, keeping you safe. And we'll do whatever we have to do to keep you away from the phone. We can't risk a leak right now."

"But I would never—"

"I know you wouldn't, but try convincing Neil of that." Clint sounded exasperated, and Marissa wondered if he'd spent considerable energy trying to do just that.

"All right. I'll play the good little citizen and do what I'm asked to do. But it better be a nice hotel. I'm still shuddering over that fleabag flophouse where you cuffed me to the bed—and I want steak for dinner—no, steak *and* lobster."

That made her think of Sophia and her "lobsta." "Has anyone talked to Sophia? Poor thing, she must be worried to death."

"Ah . . . Sophia's fine. She was taken into custody the minute she hit the airport."

"What?" Marissa's outrage returned full force. "Clint, you didn't have her arrested!"

"I had to. I have no way of knowing where her allegiance falls, where her connections are. I had to ensure that she was kept quiet. She'll be released tomorrow morning and all charges will be dropped."

"I can't believe this. After all the help we've given you—"

"And I appreciate it. But I couldn't leave anything to chance. Come on, are you ready to go? I've made reservations for us at the Doubletree."

"The one downtown? At the Allen Center?"

"That's the one."

Hmm. She supposed it could be worse. A whole night in a luxury hotel with Clint Nichols? *Oh, stop it*, she scolded herself. "Can I stop by my place and get a few things?"

"It's been taken care of."

Marissa was ominously silent during the short drive to the Doubletree. Clint couldn't really blame her. After everything she'd been through—everything he'd done to her—and all the assistance she'd given him, it didn't seem fair to treat her as if she were a suspect.

But McCormick didn't have an ounce of trust in her or her brother. His main objective wasn't so much keeping her safe as keeping her from blowing their operation with a misplaced word in someone's ear. She could even do it unintentionally. No telling which of her friends and relatives were connected.

Actually, Clint wondered if McCormick wasn't more interested in keeping him busy and distracted than in any possible breach of security. If there was one thing that might keep Clint away from the action tonight, it was a hotel with Marissa Gabriole in it.

Not that she'd have anything to do with him. She stood beside him at the registration desk, sullen and pouty. He wanted to kiss that pout off her lips.

The clerk handed him two plastic card keys. "Do you need help with your luggage?" she asked.

"No, I believe our luggage was delivered earlier."

"Oh, right, I do see that notation. Have a nice evening."

Marissa raised her eyebrows at that. "What luggage?" she asked once they were alone in the elevator.

"I'm not exactly sure, but the Bureau does have some amazing resources."

"Are we . . . sharing a room?"

"It looks less suspicious that way—I mean, it stands out less. I don't know how powerful Eddie's operation is, but I'm not discounting the fact that someone could be hunting for us. You're Mrs. Yarbrough, by the way. Cindy. I'm Max."

It gave him an unexpected twinge in his gut to think of Marissa as his wife. What a fantasy. As if he could look forward to anything so normal ever again. He would forever be a target. People like Eddie Constantine carried grudges that lasted a lifetime. He would either be looking over his shoulder the rest of his life . . . or he'd have to change jobs and move to Peoria, as Marissa had laughingly suggested the day before.

Either way, his life couldn't include Marissa. He was surprised at how depressed that thought made him. He'd known her such a short time. Yet now he couldn't take a breath without thinking about her.

He opened the door to their room, quickly noting the two double beds, as requested. As angry as Marissa was with him, he didn't imagine she'd be wanting to share.

"Oh, there really is luggage here for us," she said, staring at the two matching brocade bags lying neatly at the foot of one of the beds. "I can't wait to see what's inside," she added dryly.

Clint stood back and watched as she unzipped the first bag with trepidation. "Oops, I think this one must be yours," she said, holding up a pair of white men's briefs. "Let's try the other one." She unzipped it and threw it open. "Oh. Oh, dear."

Clint came closer to inspect the contents. Sitting on top, folded in tissue paper, was a black satin cocktail dress.

Marissa picked it up gingerly. "This is kinda flashy. Where did it come from?"

"I'm not sure."

She dug through the rest of the clothes, finding underthings, toiletries, even stockings. "Didn't they bring me any normal clothes?" she asked. "Jeans or sweats or something?" But she found nothing practical in the case—not even any shoes.

Clint's bag held a tuxedo, of all things, along with all the appropriate accoutrements. Marissa probably didn't really want to know where the stuff had come from. Last time that dress had seen daylight, it was probably on an undercover agent posing as a prostitute. No telling which gangster his tux had once belonged to, seized during some raid.

He'd asked for clean clothes, and the Bureau had outfitted them for prom night.

"At least the underwear is new," she conceded as she tore the tags off. "I'm starving, by the way. You did say something about feeding me?"

"I'll take care of dinner. Why don't you . . . take a bubble bath or something?"

"That's an excellent idea. Remember, steak and lobster. That was the deal." With that she dragged the whole suitcase with her into the bathroom and slammed the door.

Marissa had worked up a good steam, and she intended to nurse it during her bubble bath. She would think up dozens of grounds on which to sue the FBI for their treatment of her. No, wait, she thought as she dumped some almond coconut bath salts, compliments of the mysterious suitcase, into the rushing water. Revenge against the whole Bureau wasn't specific enough. It was Clint she wanted to punish.

She could always tell Neil McCormick the truth about his hotshot Special Agent Nichols, maybe arrange for Clint and Jimmy to share a cell. That would fix Clint's little red wagon.

But even that wasn't personal enough. She quickly stripped off her clothes and eased into the steaming water with a sigh of pure, contradictory delight. She supposed what she really wanted was to get even with Clint by making him feel as used and inconsequential as he'd made her feel, to let him know that their idiotic, incredible lovemaking in the laundry room hadn't meant diddly to her.

Then again, she was lying in a scented bubble bath in a luxury hotel, contemplating a lobster dinner. It was hard to stay bent out of shape under those circumstances. After all, *she* could be the one sharing jail space with Jimmy. At least they hadn't arrested her, even if they were severely hampering her constitutional freedoms.

As for Clint's cavalier treatment of her . . . hell, he was a man on a mission. He'd needed to secure her loyalty, and she knew enough about human nature to realize that the easiest way for a man to bind a woman to him was through sex. Maybe he hadn't seduced her with that purpose in mind, but it had worked, hadn't it? She'd helped him get his evidence, and she'd protected him from his own people, all because she'd forged a bond with him. Or so she'd thought.

She had to face the fact that her adventure was over now, or very nearly so. Despite her best intentions, she had strong feelings for Clint. Perhaps he wasn't devoid of some fondness for her himself. But how improbable could one relationship be?

She'd seen it, the silent apology, in the set of his mouth, and the way he wouldn't quite meet her inquiring gaze. She'd seen that look before. The "I-don't-want-to-hurt-you, but" look.

Very well, she thought as she pulled the drain stopper and reluctantly let her dreamy bath slip away. She'd pretend she wasn't hurt, even though she was. It was hard to let a man like Clint slip through her fingers as if she didn't care, but it would be harder still to admit her true feelings when she knew how impossible the situation was.

She made up her mind to try to relax and enjoy the evening. By the next morning, if she could believe what Clint had told her, she could return to her normal life.

Marissa took her time getting dressed. After the last two days of slapdash grooming, it felt wonderful to brush her teeth, comb conditioner through her hair, rub lotion into every square inch of her skin. Whoever had packed her bag hadn't included makeup, but just about any other kind of cosmetic she could dream of was there—even a nail file and cotton swabs.

She was pawing through the plastic cosmetics bag, wondering if there might be any dental floss, when she froze. It couldn't be. . . . But yes, the red plastic packet she'd stumbled across was indeed a condom.

Who had packed this bag, anyway, and on whose orders? she wondered suspiciously.

Marissa put on the surprisingly fancy underwear, rose pink with touches of black lace, then stepped into the ridiculous dress. It fit as if it had been tailor-made for her, the midnight satin hugging her breasts, waist, and hips like a lover's caress.

"Oh, my," she murmured as she inspected herself. The provocative image in the mirror wasn't what she really wanted to present to Clint. But she had little choice. It was the dress, or the clothes she'd been wearing for two days.

She tossed her head. What the hell. Give Clint an eyeful of the sultry vixen he was so willing to use and toss aside, she thought with a saucy smile.

When she opened the bathroom door, it was Marissa who got an eyeful—Clint in a tux with a wine-colored tie and cummerbund. He was shaved, and his hair was combed. He looked more like a Monte Carlo high-stakes gambler than the rugged, rough-around-the-edges renegade she'd come to know and—*and love*.

She savagely pushed that thought aside. It was ridiculous. How could she love someone she'd known only a couple of days? And even if she did, what could she do about it?

Clint looked over at her and did a double take. "Damn." His eyes practically bored holes in her.

She felt suddenly less brazen as his gaze roved over her without the slightest hesitation. "Who packed that suitcase, anyway, Strumpets R Us?"

"I'm not sure who packed the suitcases, but remind me to thank them."

She could feel her face flushing. "I can't go out in public like this, Clint. This isn't exactly my usual style."

"Well, it's a good thing we're not going out, then."

"But—"

"I called room service. Neil thinks we should keep a low profile."

"We're a little overdressed for room service," she said, perching gingerly on the edge of the bed. "But maybe it's just as well. I didn't find any dress shoes in my bag." Which struck her as odd, now that she thought about it. The Bureau had remembered condoms but forgotten shoes?

Clint could hardly believe his eyes. He'd known Marissa was beautiful, but in that black dress she was a temptress, a seductive witch.

Maybe Neil was behind the oddly packed suitcases. Hell, maybe he'd even put Marissa up to a seduction, to keep Clint pleasantly occupied over the next few hours.

Clint, however, refused to let himself be sucked in. Sure, she aroused him. Sure, he could easily lay her down right there and make love to her the way it should have been done in the first place, slowly, with sweet words and lingering kisses. Sure, he could slip those skinny little straps off her shoulders and bury his face in the lush softness of her breasts—

"Is something wrong?" Marissa asked.

"What?" He'd been staring at her, probably with his tongue hanging out.

"You were looking at me as if something was wrong. I thought maybe I had a tag showing."

"No, you're perfect." He hadn't meant for his voice to sound so husky, so adoring. "You look fine," he amended. "How about a glass of wine?" He gestured toward an ice bucket, where a bottle of Chablis nested in ice cubes, waiting to be opened. "It arrived while you were in the tub."

Marissa's eyebrows shot up. "Someone went out of their way to keep us happy and settled firmly in this room tonight. What is the Bureau afraid we'll do?"

He saw no reason not to tell her. "I've been ordered to stay away from the bust tonight."

"Oh, I see." She swung her bare feet onto the bed and stacked the two pillows behind her back. "Why would you want to be there? I mean, really. It'll be dangerous."

Clint fumbled as he tried to uncork the wine. He was so flustered by the sight of Marissa reclining on the bed that he couldn't perform even the simplest task. "For eight months I've been living and breathing this case. I spearheaded it. I organized the task force. I orchestrated every move we made. And now Neil is cutting me out of the conclusion."

"You could be killed," she said softly.

"Do you think I care about that?"

She sighed and looked so sad, it made his throat tight. "Apparently not. I'll take that wine now."

He poured two glasses half full of the golden liquid, then carried them across the room to where Marissa reclined. She appeared relaxed, but there was a certain giveaway tightness around her mouth. He handed her one goblet, then sat on the edge of the bed. Neither of them drank.

"I need some closure." If he was going to quit the Bureau, he wanted to go out with a bang. And he'd pretty much decided he needed to quit. He was burned out, over the edge. What he'd done to Marissa had proved that.

"You're going anyway," she said, each word a sharp spear of accusation. "Despite orders."

"Yeah, I guess I am."

"Figures," she muttered under her breath. Then she held her glass aloft. "Here's to testosterone." She took a long sip of her wine.

"What's that supposed to mean?"

When she answered, it was with an intensity that startled Clint. "You don't need closure. That's a bunch of bull. You just want to run around, waving your gun and being a big shot. You're afraid you won't get credit for all your hard work if you're not in the middle of the action, risking your life when it's totally unnecessary."

"You don't understand."

"I do understand. Whether you're a cop or a gangster, the motivation is the same. You all like to play your little-boy games, only you play for real. People get hurt. You think you're invincible, but bullets and bombs will break you apart as easily as a bad guy.

"Why can't you leave it alone?" Her eyes were shiny with tears. She set her wineglass aside and rubbed angrily at one eye with the heel of her hand.

Clint set his glass down, too, and took both her hands in his. "Nothing is going to happen to me."

She looked back at him defiantly. "That's exactly what my father said to me. There'd been phone calls, death threats. I answered the phone one day. It scared me. Papa told me not to worry—that he was a big man, much more important and smarter than the men making the phone calls. We were going to church. I ran back inside to get my money for the collection basket, and there was an explosion, and I never saw my parents again except in very small pieces. So don't tell me nothing will happen to you. You don't know that."

Clint felt the pain, so poignant even after all these years. He brushed one of her tears away with his thumb, but more followed. "When it comes right down to it, none of us knows when we'll leave this planet."

"But we don't have to run around doing things to hasten that moment," she argued. "Oh, never mind. You'll never listen to me, or anyone else who tells you what you don't want to hear."

"Marissa." He hated to have her dismiss him so harshly. "Do you really think I'm beyond redemption?"

"If you go to that bust tonight, if you deliberately put yourself in danger for nothing more than a thrill, then you're beyond redemption. Or at least beyond anything I can comprehend."

Or anyone she could love. She hadn't said it, but the implication was unmistakable. She was asking him to choose.

Was she right? Was it purely his ego that drove him to participate in the night's operation?

No, came the gut answer. He needed to be there for a reason. He had a feeling, a cop's sixth sense, that his presence was an essential factor. He also had a feeling—and it didn't take a genius to figure this one out—that if he and Marissa made love, it would be the last time.

He touched her face again, wetting his fingers with her tears. She didn't shy away from his hand, as he'd expected her to do. Instead she turned her head and kissed his palm.

"Marissa . . ." He wanted to warn her not to push him too far, but he couldn't find the right words.

She held his hand against her face. "Nothing I've said has changed your mind?"

He couldn't answer her. For the first time he felt a prickle of uncertainty. What was really important, anyway? Was it that crucial to finish what he'd started? A part of him needed to know what had happened, where he'd gone so wrong with Rachelle. But all that sordidness represented his past.

With a flash of insight, he realized that Marissa was his future. "All right. I'll stay."

She flashed him a smile so brilliant, it almost blinded him, but it quickly faded.

"What? What's wrong?"

"It's just that . . . well, I should have learned by now that I can't reform people, shape them to my satisfaction. It didn't work with Jimmy."

"People do change. It happens."

"People change when they truly want to, for themselves. Maybe I'm the one who needs to do some changing."

He couldn't imagine why. She was damn near perfect, as far as he was concerned.

"Never mind," she said when he started to point out her perfection. "Will you kiss me?"

He'd meant to avoid any further sexual contact with her. But there were some invitations a man couldn't turn down. He leaned closer, eliminating the few inches between them, and captured her smooth, pink lips with his.

He meant it to be a sweet kiss, a seal of his agreement to stay with her instead of crashing the bust. But it quickly escalated. He tasted the salt of her tears combined with the mellowness of the wine she'd sipped.

She reached for him and held him fast against her, and suddenly his hands were all over her, trailing against the slick silk of her dress.

Her breasts were soft, except where her pebbled nipples strained against the bodice. He grazed one of them with his thumb. Her response rippled through the entire length of her body.

He toyed with the spaghetti straps, thinking that he would do exactly as he'd imagined earlier—slip them off her shoulders and bury his face against the softness of her breasts.

He never got the chance. Someone knocked at the door. He froze, and Marissa stiffened.

"Room service," he whispered. "If we're very quiet, they'll go away."

"Coming!" Marissa trilled out, then whispered, "Uh-uh, you're not cheating me out of dinner, no matter how badly I want you out of that tux."

TWELVE

Whew, Marissa thought as a waiter rolled a cart into the room. Without the interruption, she'd have been a goner. Now, at least, she had a few minutes to organize her thoughts and decide whether she really wanted to make love to Clint a second time.

The waiter put a white cloth on a small table in the corner of the room, quickly adding china, silver, and even a crystal vase with a red rose. Then he began filling the plates, uncovering dish after dish, sending delectable odors wafting through the room.

Marissa came over to inspect the elegantly appointed table. "You really did order lobster," she said to Clint.

"Of course. That was the deal we had." He pulled some bills out of his pocket to tip the waiter, who nodded discreetly and disappeared.

Moments later, Clint came up behind her with their wineglasses, reaching around her to set them on the table. She could feel the heat of his body through the thin satin of her dress. When he scooped her hair aside and planted a warm kiss at her neck, she thought her knees would give way. It was a good thing he stopped and pulled a chair out for her. She sat down.

He claimed the other chair. "Does dinner meet with your satisfaction?"

"You know it does." Lobster tail and a petite fillet, rice pilaf with mushrooms, a cup of seafood bisque, a tomato and basil salad, and chocolate-strawberry cheesecake. It was enough to feed a third-world village. "This all seems so civilized. Hard to believe it was only yesterday morning I was handcuffed to a bed in a cheap motel, threatening to emasculate you." She dug in, using her tiny, three-pronged fork to free a succulent piece of lobster from the shell. She dipped it in melted butter and popped it into her mouth.

Clint was staring at her. "I'm not feeling all that civilized, myself," he muttered, savagely cutting into his medium-rare steak.

Marissa sampled a bit of everything. The velvety bisque was to die for, so she finished it, then picked at everything else until she was full. She drained her glass of wine, and Clint automatically refilled it.

"Thanks," she murmured, her fingertips touching his as she took back the glass. She noticed that he'd spent more time watching her eat than eating himself. She tried not to let it unnerve her, but she had the distinct impression she was being stalked. He leaned back in his chair and stared. She stared back, a deer frozen in headlights.

All right, so she'd forced him to make a difficult decision. It would be excruciating for him to watch the clock, waiting for eleven o'clock, knowing he was missing the action.

She almost owed it to him to distract him, right?

It sounded like as good a rationalization as any for what she was about to do. She delicately wiped her mouth with her napkin, then stood and stretched. And with Clint watching her expectantly, she slowly lowered the zipper on her dress. It whispered down her body into a pool of black at her feet, leaving her wearing only the pink panties.

Clint's eyebrows shot up. "Oh, my."

He'd think "oh my" when she got through with him. She would kick out the stops and put to use the full power of her seductive abilities. If a panicked coupling in a laundry room could bring them ecstasy, she shivered to imagine what heights they could reach if they worked at it. They might not ever see each other again after the night was over. But, by heavens, she intended to make it a night neither one of them would ever forget.

She walked over to him, bent down, and untied his shoes, then removed them. She ran her hands up his pants' legs. He gasped when she reached his hips. She skimmed over them, then up the front of his shirt to the bow tie. She started to untie it, then changed her mind and stood. With her hands propped on the arms of Clint's chair, she leaned forward, gripped the tie with her teeth, and yanked it untied.

"I sense a warming trend in this room," Clint said, his voice unsteady.

"Mmm, why do you think I took my clothes off?" Marissa asked as she pulled the tie free of his collar and tossed it aside. "Why don't you stand up so I can undress you?"

He nearly toppled the chair in his haste to obey her.

Marissa wasn't sure where her temptress persona came from. She'd never acted this way before. But somehow she managed to keep her cool as she dispensed with Clint's jacket, then reached around him, pressing her breasts against the crisp pleats of his shirt as she undid the cummerbund.

Clint's hands fluttered at her shoulders, but he dropped them to his sides again as she went to work on his shirt studs. It felt like an eternity passed while she struggled with the stubborn studs, but he didn't help her. He simply stood there, breathing in and out.

His shirt fell to the floor, followed by his belt. When she went for the button on his tuxedo pants, he grasped both her wrists in his. "Marissa. Just one thing." His voice was thick, husky. "We did this once already without protection. I don't want—"

"Mmm, it's a good thing your friends at the Bureau are psychic. They prepared us for any eventuality."

"You're kidding."

"No." She pulled her hands loose from his. "Back in a minute." She went into the bathroom and found the plastic packet. When she returned to the bedroom, the lights were off except for one by the bed, and Clint reclined on the bed without a stitch of clothing.

"Oh, my," she said, a little breathless, echoing his earlier sentiment. But he was a magnificent specimen to behold. She hadn't gotten the full, panoramic view in that laundry room. With her heart hammering erratically and

her palms suddenly moist, she approached slowly, not feeling quite as brazen anymore.

"Come here, Marissa. Let me make love to you the way it should have been done in the first place." He stood up and threw the covers back, then held out his arms to her.

He sounded so sincere, so . . . so loving, she thought as she went to him without a shred of hesitation. If this wasn't love, then she didn't understand the emotion. She went into his arms and they kissed, tenderly, slowly, as if it were the first time.

The kiss deepened. His tongue found hers and teased it as his hands explored her back. They felt huge, his hands, as if they could crush rocks, but they were gentle as butterfly's wings as he caressed every sensitive square inch. He moved to her bottom, exploring through the slick panties, then easing one hand beneath the elastic to cup her bare skin. Enchanted with the feel of his caress, she broke the kiss long enough to shimmy out of her panties.

When she stood up, he grasped her around the waist and pulled her to the bed. Their kissing took on a frantic quality as she tried to touch all of him at the same time— his sinewy thighs, his lightly furred chest, the cast-iron biceps. Even his ears held interest.

Finally she dared to insinuate her hands between their bodies and grasp his erection. The sense of raw power she felt was intoxicating. She was so revved, she could hardly articulate words, but she tried anyway. "Can I . . . make you ready?"

"I think I've been ready for hours." He nearly

growled between nibbles on her neck. One of his hands had found the heat between her legs. She shifted, allowing him access, then gasped when he slid one finger inside, immediately finding the most sensitive spot. "Looks like you might be ready too."

"Mmm. Oh, yes, um, I meant . . ." Oh, what was the use? Her tongue wasn't working, at least not for speech purposes. She fished the condom out from under the pillow where she'd stashed it, and ripped it open with her teeth.

"Ah." Apparently understanding had dawned. He took the package from her. "Let me."

Gladly, she thought. Her seductress routine would have fallen apart at the seams. She'd never been very good with condoms, the few times she'd tried to wrestle with them.

Not so Clint. He had himself sheathed in split seconds. Then he was on top of her, pushing against her, seeking the entrance she was more than happy to grant him.

"You're so beautiful. Have I told you that?" he said before he slid inside her.

Yes, he had, but she didn't mind hearing it again. She closed her eyes and lost herself to the incredible feelings—not only the physical sensations, but the emotions welling up, surrounding her like an aura of pure golden light.

She hooked her legs around him, letting him push deeper. His mouth found her breast, and her breathing quickened as he teased her nipple with his tongue and teeth. She buried her fingers in his thick, dark hair as the pressure inside her built to an excruciating degree, the pleasure so intense, she thought she would explode.

And then she did. She was cartwheeling through space, free-falling, complete with wind rushing past her ears and lights flashing behind her eyelids. Sensations rippled from her core through every cell down to her fingers and toes.

She was almost surprised to find herself still in bed, the echoes of her cries reverberating around the room.

"Are you quite finished?" Clint asked, kissing her forehead, then her nose, then her chin.

"Are you?" she countered.

"Ages ago. I was waiting for you to come back from whatever planet you were on."

"Oh." She'd been so caught up in her own ecstasy, she'd missed his. And, she thought glumly, when would she get another chance?

He kissed her again. "Don't look at me that way. Do you have any idea what it does to a man's ego when he actually makes a woman scream with pleasure?"

"I honestly don't know, since I've never done that before."

He seemed pleased by her answer.

He withdrew and eased himself down beside her, pulling her against his shoulder. "At a time like this, I wish I could say all the right things."

"I'm not expecting any pretty words from you, Clint."

"Just the same . . . do you remember what I said to you in the closet at the Foxhunt? Right before Eddie opened the door?"

She gave a little huff of laughter as her heart suddenly

accelerated. "That was a dying declaration. I won't hold you to it."

"Yeah, well, I'm plenty alive now, so you have to believe me when I say I'm crazy for you. I know I'm not the kind of man you would ever want in your life. I know I represent everything you despise, and I've put you through hell and threatened you and almost got you killed, so I don't anticipate this great depth of feeling from you in return. I wanted you to know that I don't take this lightly. And I'm sorry for whatever pain I've caused you."

Tears formed in Marissa's eyes, because she knew he was right, dammit. He wasn't the man for her. Not that she thought what he did with his life was wrong. He was helping put people like Eddie out of commission, and that had to count for something. But it was the way he lived that she couldn't abide. She couldn't survive loving a man who exposed himself to danger day after day.

At the same time, Clint was dead wrong. She did return his feelings, measure for measure. But it probably wasn't wise for her to tell him. He had incredible power over her. He could bind her to him with very little effort, and she'd be powerless to walk away.

She still could walk away. And she wanted that option to remain open.

The phone rang, startling her out of her reverie. God Almighty, who could be calling them? She glanced at the digital clock on the nightstand. It wasn't quite eleven. Had the bust gone down? Were they calling Clint to let him know the outcome?

Please, she prayed, let everything be okay.

━━━━◆━━━━◆━━━━

Clint rolled over and picked up the receiver as adrenaline pumped through his system. "Yeah?"

"Clint." It was Neil's voice. He didn't even bother to identify himself. "We've got a helluva mess here. When we moved in, the people from the plane thought Constantine's people had turned, and they started shooting. Then all hell broke loose. The plane took off, but it had a leaky fuel tank. Now we've got a man down and a hostage situation."

Clint said nothing, though his gut roiled. This was every agent's nightmare, a Waco in the making.

"Constantine is injured," Neil continued. "He's holed up in this barn-type building, and he's holding a woman hostage. We're at a standoff."

"Can you talk to him?"

"Yeah, communications are open. But he won't talk to anyone but you. In person."

Clint resisted the urge to say, "I told you so." He'd known, from the moment he laid eyes on that information in Eddie's safe, that he should be present at the rendezvous. He'd known it when he argued with Neil earlier that day about taking part in the operation. And he'd known it again a couple of hours earlier, when Marissa asked him to justify his participation in the bust.

Now he knew why he should've been there.

"The SOB just wants to kill me, you know," Clint said. He could feel Marissa tense at those words, though she wasn't even touching him. He reached out and gave her hand a reassuring squeeze, but he couldn't look at her. "Do you know the identity of the woman?"

"It's your ex-wife," Neil said, confirming what Clint had already suspected.

Hell, she wasn't a hostage, she was a conspirator. She was probably playing along, allowing Eddie to use her as a pawn to manipulate him. But what if she really was in danger? Eddie wasn't sentimental. Because he'd been sleeping with Rachelle didn't mean he wouldn't kill her.

"If you'd rather not get involved—"

"Oh, please, Neil," Clint said with a weary shake of his head. "As if I'd stand by while someone puts a gun to Rachelle's head. I'm a trained hostage negotiator. I'll be there in twenty minutes."

Neil gave him some terse directions on where to meet, then hung up.

Clint turned to Marissa. She was already sitting up, a pillow hugged protectively against her body. "I couldn't have planned a better way to ruin things, huh?" he said.

She didn't answer, and he didn't blame her for being mad. He'd promised her he wouldn't go. She'd made love with him because of that decision. She must feel betrayed.

"I have to go," he said.

"I know. You have to save the life of the woman who conspired to have you killed."

"That's right," he said as he climbed out of bed and went in search of his clothes. He felt suddenly self-righteous. "She's a human being, and I'll save her life if I can, regardless of what she's done. I would do the same for any woman, even if I'd never met her. That's my job, keeping people alive. That's what separates me from *them*, Marissa, from your father and Eddie and even Jimmy. I wish you'd at least try to remember that. You might not care for my methods, but you can't argue with my motives."

She sat silently watching him as he pulled on his clothes. Then, abruptly, she got up and scurried into the bathroom.

"What are you doing?" he called after her.

"Putting on my clothes. I'm coming with you."

"No, you're—"

"Yes, I am," she said with quiet authority when she came back into the room moments later wearing her old clothes. She located the canvas flats she'd been wearing earlier and stepped into them. "I will not sit here in this hotel room waiting for the phone to ring, to find out whether you're dead or alive."

"But it's dan—"

"Dammit, I know it's dangerous. That's not stopping you, and it won't stop me." She strode over to him until she was face to chest with him, then grabbed the lapels of his open shirt, stood on her toes, and looked up, practically snarling. "I'm going. Is that clear?"

He nodded. He wouldn't dream of arguing with her when she was in such a state. She might chew his leg off. Besides, he could always find a safe place to stash her once he got to the scene. Surely one of his coworkers had handcuffs.

Marissa remained silent during the drive to the mysterious airstrip. She was still in shock that Clint had allowed her to accompany him. For all her bravado, she hadn't for a minute believed that he would put aside his macho I'm-the-man attitude and let her desires prevail.

She'd meant business, though. She smiled in the darkness of the car as she remembered how she'd grabbed him by the shirt and shaken him as if she were a dog with a bone twice as big as itself. If he hadn't let her come, she'd have followed him. She'd have found a way. If he had it in mind to throw himself in front of a bullet or some other fool macho thing, she wanted to be in a position to stop him.

She'd only recently realized she loved him, and she wasn't going to lose him that quick.

"Is your job like this all the time?" she asked, breaking the silence.

"No." He didn't elaborate.

Seeing that his mind was elsewhere, she decided not to bother him. He was probably doing some mental-preparation thing for whatever was to come. He'd said something about hostage negotiating. He might be formulating strategy.

Clint stopped once to consult a city map, then drove ahead with unerring determination. Soon he turned onto a bumpy dirt road. They were in the middle of nowhere. Marissa found it hard to believe such a desolate area existed so close to Houston.

"Should be near," Clint murmured as he turned off the lights. He continued driving, though there was nothing in front of them but pitch blackness.

"Do you have night vision or something?" she asked.

"No, but Neil and company do. Infrared goggles, laser sensors, you name it. I want to make sure they see me before one of Eddie's people. Ah, there."

"What?" She hadn't seen anything.

"They signaled me with a flashlight. We can go ahead."

As they crept forward, Marissa could gradually make out the shape of a car in front of them on the road. Clint pulled up beside it and opened the window. He carried on a murmured conversation with the man in the car, then drove on.

Marissa still couldn't see much, but she could sense the tension in the air as Clint drove into a nest of vehicles—police cars, unmarked cars—and something that looked like a tank. An open-air, tentlike structure had been erected behind the shelter of the tank thing. A single electric bulb in the tent was the only light source.

A tall, stocky woman greeted Clint as he opened the door. "Nichols. The command post is over there." She pointed to the tent. "McCormick has been practically frothing at the mouth, he's so anxious to see you."

"Is it safe here?" Clint asked. "Are we beyond Eddie's firepower?"

"We think so." The woman gave Marissa a sour look. "Safest place for her would be at the command center with you. Nothing's coming through that armored truck."

Marissa was glad to hear that. She'd been afraid someone would override Clint's okay and kick her out. They still might, if she didn't keep a low profile. She tried to be inconspicuous as Clint hustled her to the tent.

Before he even greeted his boss, he pushed Marissa

into a folding chair. "Don't move, don't talk," he admonished her before turning his back and facing Neil. "What've we got?"

Neil pointed to a small video monitor set up on a plank table. "We've got an infrared camera on the truck. That's a view of the warehouse—it's a converted barn, really."

"How many are in there?"

"He says five others, but we think he's lying. We've got three of his men in custody and one on the way to the hospital. He couldn't have brought that many with him. We think it's just him and the—him and Rachelle."

"And she's a hostage?"

"They've come to the window three times, and he's had a gun to her head each time. We've talked to her— she sounds pretty scared, says Eddie's gone crazy or something."

"What kind of firepower do they have?"

"We think only one handgun. If they had anything more powerful, they'd have tried to use it. We've given them plenty of chances."

"When do I get to talk to Eddie?" Clint asked.

"Now. There's an open line." Neil pointed to a speakerphone.

Clint took a deep breath, stretched his arms over his head as if preparing for an Olympic sprint, then jabbed the talk button on the phone. "Yo, Eddie."

There was a long silence. Then, "Clint? That you, buddy boy?" Marissa recognized the voice as Eddie's, although it sounded weak, kind of breathy.

"None other," Clint replied.

"I feel I know you well, after all these months of dodging you."

"Put Rachelle on," Clint said in a no-nonsense voice. Marissa shivered. She'd heard that voice before, directed at her.

"All in due time."

"Put her on now. You've got ten seconds, or I give the order to move in and I don't care who gets hurt."

Neil frantically shook his head. Clint held up his finger, a silent signal for his boss to be patient. Marissa understood. Rachelle was the weakest link. Clint's best chance was to undermine her part in this hostage charade. And that's what it was—a charade.

"Now wait a minute, buddy boy—" Eddie began.

"Ten," Clint said calmly. "Nine."

"Okay, okay. Here she is."

Another pause, then, "Clint?" A female voice. "Oh, Clint, he's gonna kill me. Please, please, baby, do something. Do what he asks. Bring him a doctor. He's bleedin' like crazy."

"He'll get the finest medical care tax money can buy if he just surrenders," Clint said calmly. "You tell him that."

Marissa bit her nails. How could Clint remain so cool?

"He doesn't listen to me, baby."

Clint hit the mute button. "Yeah, I'll just bet."

"There's a doctor here," Neil said. "Maybe he could go in and give Eddie something to knock him out."

Clint shook his head. "Rachelle would turn the gun on him the moment anything went wrong."

Neil appeared confused. "What are you saying?"

"Rachelle isn't a hostage. She's acting."

"You're sure?"

"I'd stake my life on it. If I can keep talking to her, I can get her to surrender. I know every one of her hot buttons."

Marissa did her best to ignore the implications of that statement.

He punched the talk button again. "Rachelle?"

"That's enough chitchat with your sweetie." Eddie was back, still sounding not quite like himself. Marissa wondered how badly he was injured. If they waited long enough, he might pass out from loss of blood.

"Why'd you want to talk to me, specifically?" Clint asked.

"I thought we could work out a little trade—you for the babe."

Clint actually laughed. "What good would that do you? It's not as if you'd get out of here alive with any hostage, certainly not me. Anyway, you think I'd trade my life for Rachelle's? Dream on. She's not worth it to me. You can kill her for all I care."

"What?" Neil screamed.

Clint gave his boss a warning look, as if to say, *I know what I'm doing.* "Before you kill her, though," he continued to Eddie, "you ought to know that there are a dozen SWAT team sharpshooters aiming their rifles at that flimsy little shack you're in. If we hear even the slightest noise that might be a gun firing from your direction, my boss—and he's standing right here, nodding—will give the order to open fire."

Neil was shaking his head frantically.

Marissa was amazed. Clint knew exactly what he was doing. Eddie wasn't into martyrdom. He'd take prison over hell, and hell was exactly where he'd be going if he died.

She'd seen the brute force and physical prowess Clint's job required, but she'd never seen this side of it— the intelligence, the cunning, the finesse, and the instinct. Clint was gifted.

She felt wicked for the awful things she'd said about him, *to* him, about his chosen profession. Being an FBI agent wasn't anything like being a gangster. She'd been wrong to equate the two. The first chance she got, she would apologize. And she would tell him she loved him.

It didn't appear she would get that chance any time soon. Clint was ignoring her, as was every other man flocking around the control center. It was just as well, she decided. She was lucky to have been allowed to stay.

Eddie had been silent a long time. Most other men would have filled the silence with something, anything, but Clint simply paced and stared at the phone. He was testing Eddie's nerve.

"Clint?" It was Rachelle's voice.

"I'm here."

"Something's wrong with Eddie. He's fading in and out, and he's not making a lot of sense."

"It's the blood loss," Clint said casually. "Not enough blood to the brain. Is he hallucinating? Delusional?"

"I don't know what you call it, he's just talking crazy. He doesn't even hear me anymore."

"Then I suggest you use this opportunity to escape."

"No! I mean, he might shoot me. He's still pointing the gun at me." She paused. "Well, anyway, if I leave him, you'll kill him."

That was a telling remark, Marissa thought. Rachelle had pretty much admitted she wasn't being held against her will.

Clint softened his voice. "I give you my word, Rachelle, that we won't kill him unless he starts shooting first. If you really want to save his life, you'll encourage him to surrender. Otherwise he's going to bleed to death."

Another long pause, then, "Oh, God, Clint, he's not moving. I think he's dead!"

"Then it's over. Come out, and as soon as you're safe, we'll send in medical help."

"I'm not coming out! I've got Eddie's gun, and I'll kill anybody who comes after me, I swear it."

"Rachelle, you're making this way harder than it has to be." Clint savagely punched the mute button, then abruptly strode out of the command center.

Marissa was out of her chair in an instant. "Clint, what are you doing?" she called after him. But she knew. The idiot was going to get himself killed. She started to run after him, but immediately there were three pairs of hands holding her back.

"No, you don't," Neil said. "You couldn't stop him, anyway."

Marissa realized Neil was right. Clint had never fully believed Rachelle would help in a plot to kill him. No matter what the evidence, he still had faith in his ex-wife. Now he was going to test that faith, and there was nothing Marissa could do about it. She allowed Neil to lead her back to her chair, but she steadfastly refused to look at the video monitor. She refused to watch him die.

THIRTEEN

Clint had heard Marissa's voice behind him, but he'd steeled himself to ignore it. He knew what it would take to end this standoff, to save Rachelle's life and possibly Eddie's, if he wasn't dead already. Now that everyone realized Rachelle wasn't a hostage, her life had become a lot more expendable to the trigger-happy sharpshooters and eager-beaver young agents. But killing her wasn't necessary. He knew Rachelle, and he intended to call her bluff. She wasn't capable of killing him.

He pushed past the ring of cops and agents who stood behind their cars or boldly strolled around in bulletproof vests. No one stopped him. He strode purposefully toward the rickety wooden barn—a makeshift storage facility for contraband, he guessed—where Rachelle was holed up. Another few feet, and he'd be within pistol range.

"Nichols?" Someone was calling him through a bullhorn. "Get the hell back."

He ignored the order. What would they do to him later, pull his badge? Like he cared.

He stopped at about thirty yards. "Rachelle?" he called. "Can you hear me?"

"Yes," she called back. Her head bobbed in the window, then disappeared. "Don't you come any closer."

"I'm unarmed, sweetie. I just want to talk, and I want to see how bad Eddie is."

"All—all right. Come ahead, slowly."

That's a girl, Clint thought as he closed the distance between himself and the building. When he reached the huge double door, it opened a crack. He pushed it the rest of the way. A flashlight resting in a corner was the only illumination, casting macabre shadows on the walls. The large enclosure was almost filled, floor to ceiling, with shoe-box-size packages wrapped in plastic—hundreds and hundreds of them. Clint had never seen such a quantity of cocaine, if that's what it was.

Rachelle stood several feet away, a gun trained on Clint as he entered. "Eddie's over there," she said, nodding toward an inert figure on the floor.

Clint carefully approached Eddie, mindful that this whole thing could be a trick. But the blood was real, and there was a whole lot of it. Clint bent down and felt for a pulse in Eddie's neck. It was there, but barely.

"He's still alive," he said. "But he won't be for long unless he gets to a hospital. So what's it going to be, Rachelle? Will you have his death on your hands? How about mine?" He approached her slowly. She backed up until she was against the far wall.

"I'll kill you," she said.

"I don't believe it." Another two steps, and the gun was in reach.

A woman's scream rang out in the muggy half-light of the barn, but it wasn't Rachelle's. It came from behind, from the door. The noise distracted Rachelle for the split second Clint needed. She turned and pointed the gun away from him. He reached out and snagged it. The moment she realized the balance of power had shifted, she crumpled.

"Oh, Clint, I'm so glad you're here. It was awful. Eddie made me do it. He was going to kill me—"

"Save it for the trial," he said harshly as he grabbed her by the arm and twisted it behind her none too gently. Only when he had her firmly under control did he turn toward the door, toward the scream.

"Marissa?" He couldn't believe it! But there she was, standing brazenly in the doorway. "What are you— How did you—" He stopped, collected his thoughts. "Ease back out that door, slowly. Keep your hands in plain sight. I don't want any last-minute heroes taking you out by mistake. I'm right behind you."

The aftermath took longer than the actual siege had taken. Marissa, who'd previously been ignored, invisible, suddenly became the focus of Neil McCormick's unwelcome attention. She'd been hustled away from the action, isolated, not even allowed to speak to Clint, which was just as well. Maybe her anger would cool before she confronted him.

Back at FBI headquarters, in a tiny interrogation

room, she explained what had happened over and over to Neil. She'd been sitting obediently in her folding chair at the command center, peeking at the video monitor. When she realized Clint, the idiot, had actually gone into that warehouse unarmed to face a couple of crazy people with guns, and no one seemed to be doing anything about it, she'd decided she couldn't sit idly by.

No one had been paying her the slightest bit of attention, so she'd calmly risen, left the command center, and melted into the darkness around them. She'd been halfway to the warehouse before anyone noticed her, and by then it had been too late to stop her.

When she arrived and peeked through the doorway, she'd seen Rachelle holding the gun practically shoved in Clint's chest, and she'd done what now seemed like the stupidest thing in the world—she'd screamed. As it turned out, she'd provided exactly the distraction Clint had needed to overpower Rachelle. Somehow, she doubted he would shower her with appreciation.

After a couple of hours, Marissa's eyelids were drooping and her words were starting to lean toward incoherence. She was also beginning to despise Neil McCormick.

"I know you have this driving need to settle every detail before sunrise," Marissa said, trying not to sneer, "but would it be too much trouble to get me some coffee? An injection of caffeine, and I might be able to go another few hours."

Neil wasn't amused by her sarcasm. He sighed as he stood up. "I'll see if I can find you some coffee." He left her blissfully alone.

A few minutes later, the door opened again and a man

walked in with a foam cup full of a steaming liquid. It took a few moments to realize the man was much taller and broader through the shoulders than Neil.

"Clint!" She didn't know whether to jump up and hug him or slap him silly. She settled for folding her arms and glaring.

He set the coffee on the table beside her, then pulled a chair uncomfortably close. "Let's talk."

"I've done enough talking tonight, thanks," she said primly, taking a sip of the black coffee. It had to be the worst coffee she'd ever tasted. "Good Lord, do you drink this stuff on a daily basis? No wonder your brain is fried. This stuff is more corrosive than battery acid."

"*My* brain? Who is it that escaped police protection and ran into the middle of a hostage situation without a clue?"

"How does it feel when someone you care about risks their life for no good reason?" she countered.

"I had a good reason, a plan, a strategy. I've known Rachelle for nine years. She wouldn't have killed me. I took the only course of action that could have saved her life, and Eddie's too. Now they'll both be around for trial. You, on the other hand, had no idea what you were stumbling into. And yes, it felt lousy," he added.

"Eddie's okay?" she asked.

"Still alive, last I heard. Our man who got shot is okay, too, just a flesh wound. Oh, and the airplane ran out of fuel a few miles over the Gulf. The Coast Guard picked them up."

"Then the operation was a success!"

"By certain standards. But let's not change the subject. We could file charges against you for interfering with a police investigation, you know."

"Clint, really! Is that supposed to scare me, after everything that could have happened?" When he continued to glare at her, she decided a little humble pie was in order. "All right, so maybe it wasn't the smartest thing I've ever done. But I knew I had to help, if I could. I couldn't stand there and watch the man I love commit suicide."

"You're damned right it wasn't smart—what did you just say?"

She smiled faintly. "You heard me. I'm not crazy about your job, but I think there's room for compromise there."

He stared at her for a few tense seconds. Then he grabbed her by the shoulders and kissed her senseless, long enough to make her dizzy. "You mean it, Marissa? You think you can stand me?"

She shrugged and looked down at her lap. "I guess I could work on being more tolerant and having a little more faith, if you'll work on not trying to kill yourself on a daily basis."

"That sounds fair," Clint said, his eyes sparkling with mischief.

"Then, yes, I'm willing to try. Either that, or I'd be kicking myself the rest of my life, wondering why I let you get away."

Clint put his hand behind her head and kissed her again, more gently this time. Marissa felt herself melting into a puddle of acquiescence, and she would have made it there, too, if the door to the interrogation room hadn't opened again.

They pulled apart abruptly. Neil stepped in, grinning like a Cheshire cat. "You two might remember there's a one-way mirror looking into this room."

Marissa gasped. Clint, to his credit, at least looked uncomfortable.

"I'm finished with you both for the night. But I think you should know that our security risk people don't think either one of you is safe. There's at least one person on the outside who'd like to see you both dead. We've received some threatening phone calls . . . claiming some very strange things, I might add."

Clint and Marissa exchanged a look.

"He had an odd, high-pitched laugh. Ring any bells?"

Rusty! Marissa looked at Clint to see if he would surrender any information about Rachelle's brother.

Clint shook his head.

"We can get you transferred to another field office, Clint. Say, Butte, Montana?"

Clint grimaced. "That's okay, Neil. I think I'll be taking a leave of absence, maybe a permanent one. I've saved up some money, and I was thinking of buying a charter sailboat out in California, maybe Baja."

Neil's smile faded. "That sounds . . . nice." He switched his gaze to Marissa. "What about you, Ms. Gabriole? You'll probably be required to testify at the trial, but until then I'd recommend you leave the area."

"What, you guys won't protect her?" Clint exploded.

"If she insists on staying in Houston, we'll do what we

can, but it's not an ideal situation." He turned back to Marissa. "Any family you can stay with?"

"I don't have any family except for Jimmy," she said. "But that's okay, I was thinking of moving out of Houston anyway. I can run my little accounting business from anywhere . . . even a boat in Baja."

Clint raised his eyebrows. He actually looked hopeful.

Neil smirked. "We can work out the details later. For a couple of days, anyway, you can keep the Doubletree room. I'll figure it into the budget somehow." He stood and started to leave, but Clint halted him with one last question.

"Um, Neil, there's this family of fishermen who had their boat stolen. If there's anything the Bureau could do, you know, to help them out, I'd really appreciate it."

Neil closed his eyes and put his finger and thumb at the bridge of his nose, as if he was getting a really bad headache. "I don't even want to know what that's about." He left the room.

Clint looked at Marissa. "I thought you'd never set foot on a boat again."

"Oh, I might . . . for the right incentive."

"How about a marriage license?"

Now Marissa was speechless. Did she dare tell him she'd have settled for great sex and a year's supply of Dramamine? Nah. "If that was a proposal, this is a yes." She climbed into his lap, put her arms around him, and kissed him for all she was worth. From somewhere distant—or perhaps on the other side of the mirror—she heard a cheer go up.

THE EDITORS' CORNER

What do you get when you pit the forces of nature against the forces of man? You'll have a chance to find out after reading the four fantastic LOVE-SWEPTs coming your way next month. Two couples face the evil forces in their fellow man while the other two do battle with nature in the form of a snowstorm and a hurricane. The result is four mind-blowing romances that'll leaving you cheering—or crying—at the end!

Loveswept favorite Charlotte Hughes dazzles us with **JUST MARRIED . . . AGAIN**, LOVE-SWEPT #902. Ordered by the family doctor to take time off, Michael Kelly decides to spend Thanksgiving in his mountain cabin, away from the pressures of work. Maddie Kelly wants to spend the holiday in *her* mountain cabin, away from her well-meaning family and friends. Unfortunately, it's the same cabin. Since their separation nearly a year earlier, Maddie and Michael have been avoiding each other. When a sudden case of amnesia and a snowstorm trap them in the mountains, together with two dogs and a stowaway nephew, the couple have no choice but to endure each other's company. As they get to know each other and the unhappy people they've become, they slowly realize that what tore them apart the first time around could be the very thing that binds them together. Charlotte is at her all-time best in this touching novel of love rediscovered.

In the land of **SMOKE AND MIRRORS,** Laura Taylor paves the way for two lost souls in LOVE-SWEPT #903. Anxious to begin a new life, Bailey Kincaid fled from Hollyweird with divorce papers in hand. As co-owner and president of Kincaid Drilling, she's responsible for the safety of her men, and she's determined to make the person who is sabotaging her job site pay. When Patrick Sutton found himself interested in the shy wife of one of his clients, he immediately distanced himself from her. He's stunned to find out the woman who captured his attention years ago is now the strong-willed woman in charge of the construction on his property. Patrick had taught her how it felt to ache for something she could never have, and it hadn't been easy to get him out of her system. He insists that they were never strangers and that they deserve to follow where their hearts seem determined to lead. But can the sorrow that haunted their nights finally be put to rest? Laura Taylor writes a memorable story of fated lovers who discover the great gift of second chances.

In **ONLY YESTERDAY,** LOVESWEPT #904, Peggy Webb teases us with a timeless romance that knows no bounds. A sense of *knowing*, a sense of belonging, and a sense of love have kept Ann Debeau in Fairhope, Alabama. When she haggles with Colt Butler over a charming clock, she's pleasantly surprised at the attraction she feels for the handsome stranger. Sorting through her grandmother's belongings in the attic, Ann Debeau finds a stack of love letters addressed to a man she's never heard of. A hurricane strands her there with the waters swirling ever higher, and Colt comes to her rescue, only to be stuck right alongside her. As they read the letters, a mysterious force whisks them in time to a place where both have been before and into a relationship that was never consummated. In the past, Colt and Ann find a ghost that demands closure and an enduring love that refuses to give up on forever. Peggy Webb challenges us to believe in destiny and reincarnation, in this jewel of a Loveswept.

And in **LOVING LINDSEY,** LOVESWEPT #905, Pat Van Wie introduces neighboring ranchers and one-time best friends Lindsey Baker and Will Claxton. Years ago, a misunderstanding drove Will from Willowbend, Wyoming, but he's always known that one day he would return to the land he loves best. Never one to desert a lady in need, he offers Lindsey help in sorting out the trouble at her ranch. Though he swears he's looking to buy his land back from her fair and square, Lindsey's sure that Will is the one responsible for the "accidents." When one night of promises in the moonlight leads to more than just kisses, the dueling ranchers realize they're not just fighting for her land. In the end, will the face of her betrayer belong to the man she's dreamed of for so long . . . or the man she's trusted for all of her life? Pat Van Wie proves once more that those we love first are so often those we love forever.

Happy reading!

With warmest wishes,

Susann Brailey   Joy Abella

Susann Brailey   Joy Abella

Senior Editor   Administrative Editor

P.S. Look for these women's fiction titles coming in September! Now available in paperback from *New York Times* bestselling author Iris Johansen is **AND THEN YOU DIE. . . .** When photojournalist Bess Grady witnesses a nightmarish experiment conducted by international conspirators, she vows to do whatever it takes to stop their deadly plan from succeeding. Nationally bestselling author Katherine O'Neal pens **WRITTEN IN THE STARS,** an enthralling tale of lost treasure and found love in turn-of-the-century London and Egypt. And finally, in **CHARMED AND DANGEROUS** by Jane Ashford, a British spy finds his life turned upside down by an ex-governess whose passion for intrigue matches his own. And immediately following this page, preview the Bantam women's fiction titles on sale in August.

For current information on Bantam's women's fiction, visit our website at the following address:
http://www.bdd.com/romance

Don't miss these extraordinary books
from Bantam's women's fiction!

On sale in August:

INTO THE WILDERNESS
by Sara Donati

THE CHALICE AND THE BLADE
by Glenna McReynolds

BODY AND SOUL
by Susan Krinard

THE LONG SHOT
by Michelle Martin

LADY RECKLESS
by Leslie LaFoy

Weaving a vibrant tapestry of fact and fiction, *Into the Wilderness* sweeps us into another time and place . . . and into the heart of a forbidden, incandescent affair between a spinster Englishwoman and an American frontiersman. Here is an epic of romance and history that will captivate readers from the very first page.

INTO THE WILDERNESS
by Sara Donati

"You've never been kissed, have you?" The white cloud of his breath reached out to touch her face. His hands jerked at his sides but he kept them where they were. Now she would tell him to mind his own business, and he could put this woman out of his head.

"Why?" said Elizabeth, raising her eyes to his with a critical but composed look. "Do you intend to kiss me?"

Nathaniel pulled up abruptly and laughed. "The thought crossed my mind."

Her eyes narrowed.

"*Why* do you want to kiss me?"

"Well," Nathaniel said, inclining his head. "You seem set on going back to England, and the Mahicans say that you should never return from a journey the same person."

"How very thoughtful of you," she said dryly. "How *benevolent*. But please, do not discommode yourself, on my account." She began to turn away, but Nathaniel caught her by the upper arm.

"Now I for one hope you don't rush off," he said. "But I want to kiss you, either way."

"Do you?" she said tersely. "Perhaps I don't want to kiss you."

"I didn't mean to get you mad," Nathaniel said softly.

"What did you mean to do, then? Have some fun at my expense, but not so much that I would actually notice that you were making a fool of me?"

"No," he said, and Elizabeth was relieved to see all trace of teasing leave his face. "I'd like to see the man who could make a fool of you. I meant to kiss you, because I wanted to. But if you don't like the idea—"

She pulled away from him, her face blazing white. "I never said that. You don't know what I want." Then, finally, she blushed, all her frustration and anger pouring out in pools of color which stained her cheeks bluish-gray in the faint light of the winter moon.

"So," Nathaniel said, a hint of his smile returning. "You do want to kiss me."

"I want you to stop talking the matter to death," Elizabeth said irritably. "If you hadn't noticed, you are embarrassing me. Perhaps you don't know much about England—I don't know why you should, after all—but let me tell you that there's a reason I am twenty-nine years of age and unkissed, and that is, very simply, that well-bred ladies of good family don't let men kiss them. Even if they want to be kissed, and women do want to be kissed on occasion, you realize, although we aren't supposed to admit that. To be perfectly honest with you"—she drew a shaky breath—"I can't claim that anyone has ever shown an interest in me at home—at least, not enough interest that this particular issue would ever raise its head. Now." She looked up at him with her mouth firmly set. Her voice had lowered to a hoarse whisper, but still she looked about the little glen nervously, as if someone might overhear this strange and unseemly conversation. "You'll forgive me if I question why you would be thinking of kissing me."

"It's a wonder," Nathaniel said. "How purely stupid Englishmen can be. Scairt off from a pretty face—don't you scowl that way, maybe nobody ever thought to tell you before, but you are pretty—because there's a sharp mind and a quick tongue to go along with it. Well, I'm made of tougher stuff."

"Why—" Elizabeth began, sputtering.

"Christ, Boots, will you stop talking," said Nathaniel, lowering his mouth to hers; she stepped neatly away.

"I think not," she said. "Not tonight."

Nathaniel laughed out loud. "Tomorrow night? The night after?"

"Oh, no," Elizabeth said, trying halfheartedly to turn away. "I cannot—pardon me, I must get back."

"Back to England?" he asked, one hand moving down until he clasped a mittened hand. "Or just back to your father?"

"It isn't right that my father misrepresented things to me, that he brought me here under false pretenses, that he made plans for me that I want no part of."

"You don't want Richard Todd," Nathaniel prompted.

"No," Elizabeth said fiercely, and her eyes traveled down to focus on his mouth. "I don't want Richard Todd. I want my school."

"I will build you a school."

"I want to know why you're so angry at my father, what he's done to you."

"I'll tell you that if you really want to know," he said. "But someplace warmer."

"I don't want to get married."

He raised an eyebrow. "Then I won't marry you."

Her eyes kept darting over his face, between his mouth and his eyes, and back to his mouth, the curve of his lip. He saw this, and he knew she was thinking about kissing him. Nathaniel knew that this was a conflict for her, one not easily reconciled: she did not want marriage, and in her world—in this world—there could not be one without the other. This struggle was clear on her face, and as he expected, training and propriety won out: she was not quite bold enough to ask for the kisses she wanted. This disappointed him but he was also relieved. He didn't know how long he could keep his own wants firmly in hand. And this was not a woman who could be rushed.

"I want . . . I want . . ." She paused and looked down.

"Do you always get everything you want?" Nathaniel asked.

"No, " she said. "But I intend to start."

A runaway bride . . .
A sorcerer in disguise . . .
A spellbinding adventure
of passion and magic . . .

THE CHALICE AND
THE BLADE
by Glenna McReynolds

*In a land of forbidding castles, sacred prophecies,
and unholy betrayals, mystery surrounds the one
woman who holds the key to an ancient legacy.
She is Ceridwen, an orphan unaware of her im-
mense power—until fate leads her from a se-
cluded abbey into the tower of a feared sorcerer.*

*Dain Lavrans has no magic in himself, only
the secrets of medicine he uncovered while a soldier in the Crusades. But he finally beholds true
enchantment in the spell of passion innocently
woven by the ethereal Ceridwen. Yet there are
many who seek the maiden, all meaning to wrest
her power for themselves. Now Ceridwen and
Dain must struggle to escape the snares set by
friend and foe alike, even as they discover a love
that promises to bind them forever.*

"A stunning epic of romantic fantasy."
—*Affaire de Coeur* (five-star review)

The bestselling author of *Prince of Shadows* and *Twice a Hero* again displays her incredible talent and imagination in an enchanting new romance about a love so deep it will bring a man and a woman together . . . in another century, in another life.

BODY AND SOUL

by bestselling author

Susan Krinard

Jesse Copeland, an expert in mountain rescues, has returned to Manzanita after years in the Peace Corps. Despite an indomitable courage that sent her rappelling down cliffs, she is haunted by the nightmares and shadowy half memories surrounding her mother's mysterious death. Now she is determined to find out if her mother's "accident" was murder. What she finds instead is a man as transparent as air—sensual, muscular, his blue eyes burning into hers as she cries out one word from a place deep within her: David.

David Ventris, Lord Ashthorpe, late of His Majesty's Light Dragoons, is, simply put, a ghost. He's waited two centuries to be called back to earth by the woman he wronged. He knew her as "Sophie," a wondrous lady who sparked a passion so blazing that time could not dim the flames. Now he is being given the chance to guard her from danger and get back his soul—if only she will believe him real and not madness. If only she will love him enough to create a miracle . . . and give him life again.

"The reading world would be a happier place if more paranormal romance writers wrote as well as Krinard."—*Contra Costa Sunday Times*

"David!"

The cry echoed in his mind as he crossed through the portals between life and death and found himself in the World again. Even before he became aware of the faint shape of his own body, of the unfamiliar room around him, he knew he was Back.

He knew it wasn't 1815, nor even the century into which he'd been born. He'd known it before his own name had summoned him to the earthly plane. But not one of his temporary visitors had made him feel how long he'd been gone, or how much he'd lost.

She did.

She no longer cried out but tossed on her narrow bed, throwing the sheets from her body. Her back was turned to him, sweetly curved, the bedclothes just brushing the swell of her hips. In the morning light he could see that her hair was nearly straight, falling a few inches below her shoulders, cut simply and left uncovered to tangle about her head as she slept. It was golden in color; guinea-gold, begging a man to touch the thick strands.

Her body, petite and compact, was clothed in something like a man's nightshirt. Fine-boned hands clutched at her pillow as if it were a lifeline.

Recklessly he sat down on the edge of the bed, feeling it give under his weight. "Well, my lady?" he whispered, his voice hoarse with long disuse. "We gamble for high stakes, you and I, and I don't know all the rules of the game." She'd called him; he knew she'd be able to see him, that he could speak to her and be heard. But how would she react to the presence of a ghost?

He skimmed his hand a hairsbreadth above her

hip. "Who are you?" he asked. "Will you remember?"

But he willed her not to. Not until he found the way to make her believe in him, accept him, trust him as a benevolent visitor. A spirit, perhaps, come to help her in her earthly tribulations. He would learn what she most wanted to believe and use it to his advantage.

And then, when the time was right, he would tell her the truth—just enough to fulfill the conditions of his unearthly bargain. Enough to get what he wanted.

He smiled bitterly. "I give you fair warning, my lady," he said. "I haven't changed. I never change."

He hadn't meant her to hear him, but she did. And this time when she opened her eyes they centered directly on him.

He acted on instinct, willing himself to insubstantiality. He snapped to his feet and retreated across the room.

The woman blinked and sat up, body rigid with shock. Her gaze swept back and forth across the place where he stood, searching for what she could no longer see.

"Oh, my God," she said. She put shaking hands to her mouth, then to her cheeks. She squeezed her eyes shut and massaged her temples fiercely.

"Dreams," she muttered. "That's all it is."

But her skin was very pale, and her fingers trembled as she fumbled for a smooth, narrow object on the table beside her bed.

David knew she'd seen him. She'd seen him and was afraid, as anyone would be afraid to find a ghost at her bedside.

In the engaging tradition of Susan Elizabeth Phillips, Michelle Martin, author of *Stolen Moments*, presents a delightful cast of characters in a story about two best friends—and one man. . . .

THE LONG SHOT

by the irresistibly funny

Michelle Martin

When self-made millionaire Cullen Mackenzie returns to the Blue Ridge foothills of his childhood, he's ready to put a ring on the finger of his future bride, the beautiful and sexy Whitney Sheridan. But instead of Cullen's ring, Whitney's got a handful of eligible men wrapped around her finger—and she's not about to jump at Cullen's proposal.

Cullen turns to Samantha Lark to help him change Whitney's mind. Sam knows that nothing will get her best friend's attention faster than having another woman in the picture, so she and Cullen publicly feign love for each other. But the Great Plot sparks more than Whitney's attention—it fuels a passion that Sam and Cullen never knew existed. Whitney, though, is not about to go down without a fight. And all is fair in love and war. . . .

"I've warmed up the audience, so on with the show," she murmured as she stepped so naturally into his arms. She raised her voice so the couples nearby could easily eavesdrop as she launched into a survey of foreign cuisines she and Cullen both liked, European cities they both loved, and romantic movies that turned them both to mush.

But Cullen was distracted by the stunning discovery that Sam had curves that knew how to move caressingly into him and around him and against him. When had she gotten curves? When had she learned to move like this and look like this and smile so seductively? How could his childhood chum feel so womanly and desirable and delicious in his arms?

"Cullen, pay attention!" Sam hissed.

"Hm?" Cullen said, and then hurriedly regrouped. "Oh, sorry, Sam. What's my line?"

"I've just been complimenting your dancing. So say something about me."

Cullen's smile grew. The Great Plot was turning out to be a whole lot easier than he had imagined. "Careful, Miss Lark," he said, raising his voice, "dancing like that could get you arrested."

"For what?"

"For looking like you know exactly what to do with a man when you get him alone."

"But I do know! I'm not the kid of your golden childhood, Mr. Mackenzie. I'm all grown up."

"And a lovely job you made of it, too."

"Why, Mr. Mackenzie! Are you flirting with me?"

"No, no. Only telling truths."

"Now you sound like Noel."

"There's no need to be insulting."

She laughed. It went all the way up into her luminous brown eyes and stopped his heart for a moment. "You really must get over thinking that Noel is any kind of competition for the best man Virginia ever bred."

"And *you* should consider registering yourself in that dress as a lethal weapon."

She grinned up at him, dazzling him. "I don't think the girl who once put a frog down your back could ever make you putty in her hands."

"Oh, Miss Lark, you'd be surprised." He looked around the ballroom. "Where's a frog when you really need one?"

She laughed. "No need to panic. I've developed much more sophisticated ways of conveying my affection." She dragged him to a stop in the middle of the dance and dropped him into a dip. "Come with me to the Casbah," she said in a hideous French accent. "We will make beautiful music together!"

"Not if my back goes out on me," Cullen gasped as the couples dancing around them laughed, staring openly at these antics. Cullen was laughing, too, and realizing in the middle of the Mackenzie ballroom, and Sam's dip, just how much fun he was having. And when was the last time he had really had fun?

The dance ended, to be immediately replaced by a merengue. Sam placed a hand on his shoulder and slithered around him in a blatantly erotic fashion that was hypnotizing. She had promised to put on a show tonight and she was making a good job of it. Too good.

"Well?" she said when she stopped in front of him again, her arms resting on his shoulder.

Time stopped. His gaze never leaving her face, Cullen took her hand in his and then slid his other hand slowly across the silky warmth of her bare back and pulled her against him, loving the heat of her body and the slight tremor that rippled through her. He loved that she felt fluid and lyrical when he began dancing with her, hip to hip. She was a heady combination of fire and delicacy, silliness and strength. He loved staring down into brown eyes that never shied from his. He loved that she ran the fingers of one hand through his hair, dislodging the ponytail tie, setting his hair free.

"I've always wanted to do that," she murmured.

Sam's habit of making it hard for anyone to know when she was serious held full sway. Was this an act or was it for real? Cullen didn't know. He only knew in the strange haze of the small circle they had claimed on the dance floor that it was shocking to feel her body pressed evocatively against his, and to stare down into her flirtatious smile, to be hyper-conscious of her touch as he guided her into chassés, pivots, and maxixe rocks as if they had danced together always, when in fact—now that he thought about it—they had never danced together, even though they had known each other forever.

At his parents' parties and balls, he had danced with Whitney most of the time, and with some of the daughters of his parents' friends as a courtesy to them. But he hadn't danced with Sam. They had talked together, drunk champagne together, joked together, but never danced togther. Until now. Until this moment that he was enjoying much too much . . . and perhaps that was the reason they had never danced before.

LADY RECKLESS
by Leslie LaFoy

*Glynis Muldoon is a hardworking cattle rancher from the
windswept prairies of Kansas until a single long leap of her
horse sets her down in 1832 Ireland and into the middle of
a band of rebels. Carrick des Marceaux, a rogue Irishman
with a bounty on his head, knows who's responsible for her
magical arrival, but he's too busy evading the hangman's
noose to worry. Stranded in time, Glynis must find a way
to convince Carrick to help her return to her own time. As
the two flee across Ireland, dodging British troops and
searching for the one person with the key, they are locked in
a struggle for survival. A struggle for their love, a struggle
ultimately against fate itself . . .*

Glynis shivered. With one hand she reached up to
snap closed the upper portion of her coat and then
drew her hat down low across her brow. On the other
side of the valley, she saw her uncle pause at the crest
of the ridge. He motioned for her to come along and
she waved in acknowledgment.

"Okay, Bert," she chided her skittish horse. "One
more time. And let's get it right, okay? We're going
down this hill and up the next."

As the horse backed up, she wheeled him sharply
to the left, brought him around, and then pressed her
heels into his flanks. "Yah!"

He leaped forward and Glynis smiled in satisfaction. Her sense of victory came to a sudden end when, halfway down the ridge, the wind blasted through the valley and the skies opened up. Bert plunged down through the blinding sheets of cold, silver rain as though pursued by demons.

Despite his speed, by the time they reached the center of the valley, streams of rain were pouring off the brim of her Stetson and the water had found its way beneath her leather chaps. She clenched her teeth against the cold and reminded herself how fast this kind of deluge could create flash floods. The ridge ahead would offer some protection once she reached the top and dropped down the other side.

Beneath her the Appaloosa's muscles suddenly bunched and Glynis, sensing his intent, leaned forward and rose slightly in the stirrups. God only knew what he intended to jump, but she couldn't see through the rain and knew better than to fight his instincts. They sailed up, and even as she marveled at the length of his leap, they returned to earth with a dull ring of steel horseshoe against stone. Knowing she needed to pick the quickest way to the top of the ridge or risk being caught in fast water when the draw turned into a muddy sluice, Glynis settled back into the saddle and lifted her head to sight on the hill ahead.

There was no hill.

On sale in September:

AND THEN YOU DIE

by Iris Johansen

WRITTEN IN THE STARS

by Katherine O'Neal

CHARMED AND DANGEROUS

by Jane Ashford

Bestselling Historical Women's Fiction

⚹AMANDA QUICK⚹

____28354-5 SEDUCTION ...$6.50/$8.99 Canada

____28932-2 SCANDAL ....$6.50/$8.99

____28594-7 SURRENDER ....$6.50/$8.99

____29325-7 RENDEZVOUS ....$6.50/$8.99

____29315-X RECKLESS ....$6.50/$8.99

____29316-8 RAVISHED ....$6.50/$8.99

____29317-6 DANGEROUS ....$6.50/$8.99

____56506-0 DECEPTION ....$6.50/$8.99

____56153-7 DESIRE ....$6.50/$8.99

____56940-6 MISTRESS ....$6.50/$8.99

____57159-1 MYSTIQUE ....$6.50/$7.99

____57190-7 MISCHIEF ....$6.50/$8.99

____57407-8 AFFAIR ....$6.99/$8.99

⚹IRIS JOHANSEN⚹

____29871-2 LAST BRIDGE HOME ...$5.50/$7.50

____29604-3 THE GOLDEN

    BARBARIAN ....$6.99/$8.99

____29244-7 REAP THE WIND .....$5.99/$7.50

____29032-0 STORM WINDS ....$6.99/$8.99

Ask for these books at your local bookstore or use this page to order.

Please send me the books I have checked above. I am enclosing $____ (add $2.50 to cover postage and handling). Send check or money order, no cash or C.O.D.'s, please.

Name _____

Address _____

City/State/Zip _____

Send order to: Bantam Books, Dept. FN 16, 2451 S. Wolf Rd., Des Plaines, IL 60018
Allow four to six weeks for delivery.
Prices and availability subject to change without notice.   FN 16 6/98

Bestselling Historical Women's Fiction

IRIS JOHANSEN

____28855-5 THE WIND DANCER . . .$5.99/$6.99
____29968-9 THE TIGER PRINCE . . .$6.99/$8.99
____29944-1 THE MAGNIFICENT
                    ROGUE . . . .$6.99/$8.99
____29945-X BELOVED SCOUNDREL .$6.99/$8.99
____29946-8 MIDNIGHT WARRIOR .$6.99/$8.99
____29947-6 DARK RIDER . . . .$6.99/$8.99
____56990-2 LION'S BRIDE . . . .$6.99/$8.99
____56991-0 THE UGLY DUCKLING. . .$6.99/$8.99
____57181-8 LONG AFTER MIDNIGHT.$6.99/$8.99
____10616-3 AND THEN YOU DIE.... $22.95/$29.95

TERESA MEDEIROS

____29407-5 HEATHER AND VELVET .$5.99/$7.50
____29409-1 ONCE AN ANGEL . . . . . .$5.99/$7.99
____29408-3 A WHISPER OF ROSES .$5.99/$7.99
____56332-7 THIEF OF HEARTS . . . . .$5.50/$6.99
____56333-5 FAIREST OF THEM ALL .$5.99/$7.50
____56334-3 BREATH OF MAGIC . . . .$5.99/$7.99
____57623-2 SHADOWS AND LACE . . .$5.99/$7.99
____57500-7 TOUCH OF ENCHANTMENT. .$5.99/$7.99
____57501-5 NOBODY'S DARLING . . .$5.99/$7.99

Ask for these books at your local bookstore or use this page to order.

Please send me the books I have checked above. I am enclosing $____ (add $2.50 to cover postage and handling). Send check or money order, no cash or C.O.D.'s, please.

Name _____

Address _____

City/State/Zip _____

Send order to: Bantam Books, Dept. FN 16, 2451 S. Wolf Rd., Des Plaines, IL 60018
Allow four to six weeks for delivery.
Prices and availability subject to change without notice.   FN 16 6/98